THE DJINN'S DESIRE

A STEAMY FANTASY ROMANCE

TAMSIN LEY

Twin Leaf Press

Cover by Tamsin Ley

Copyright © 2017 Twin Leaf Press
All rights reserved.
ISBN: 1547181184
ISBN-13: 978-1547181186

Twin Leaf Press
PO Box 672255
Chugiak, AK 99567

*T*anika Skye jiggled the lock on the accordion grate protecting the salon and gave it a good hard kick before the bolts slid free. Using her full weight, she shoved the screen aside. On the cracked plate-glass door, the Seance Salon's logo had been hand-painted in bright pink letters around a rendering of a gold crystal ball with a comb and pair of scissors. The remaining glass on both the door and the large window had been painted black to hide the interior from prying eyes.

She picked up her basket of towels and entered the dusky shop, a small bell above the door frame jingling. The overheads flickered on with an annoying electric buzz, revealing two beat-up hairdresser chairs and their accompanying plate mirrors, a pair of folding chairs next to a magazine rack for waiting customers—which she never had—and a small area at the back surrounded by a threadbare velvet curtain where she did psychic readings. The scent of permanent-wave solution cloyed the air, directing Tanika's gaze to the hair sink; Birdie had once again neglected to wash the hair-rollers from her last client.

Or the water'd been shut off. Either was possible.

Much as Tanika loved this place, sometimes she wondered exactly what she was proving by keeping it open. Dropping her basket of clean towels into Birdie's station chair, she moved to the sink and turned the faucet to hot. To her relief, a solid stream of water emerged. She checked the black-cat wall clock Birdie had bought on a whim, saying it fit to have a witchy bit of decoration in the salon. Seven-fifty a.m. If she hurried, she could get the rollers cleaned before her first reading this morning and air out the stink. The chemicals didn't mix well with the scented candles she used during her readings.

The soft jingle of the store's bell drew her attention, and she turned, hoping for a walk-in. No one was there. She pressed her lips together and returned to washing the rollers. Sometimes if she ignored his antics, he went away. The water she was running sputtered and turned icy. *Dammit.* Cringing, she kept washing.

Then the lights went out.

With a sigh, she settled back and glared at the dark wall in front of her. "Fucking poltergeist."

In response, the lights flickered back on. The nearby velvet curtain rippled, and a scrawny, bare-chested man stepped through it. Not around it. Through it. His voice sounded just as emaciated as his body. "I told you not to call me that."

She dumped the curlers into a strainer and turned to face him. "Then stop fucking acting like one."

He tilted his head, the craggy lines on his face attempting a pleasant smile. "You know how to get rid of me."

"Nope. I keep telling you. You die with me." She'd been saying this so many years, the words no longer even gave her a twinge of regret.

His visage turned into a snarl, purple djinn magic sparking in his eyes. "What do you care what happens to me? Your wish has already been paid for. Just embrace it and live out your happy little mortal existence while you still have time."

Tanika's stomach churned, just as it did during each of these interactions for the previous fourteen years. In truth, she wanted to do exactly what he suggested. Create a stable home with a family to love. A little girl's dream. One she'd eschew forever if it meant the demon —he called himself a djinn, but to her he'd always be a demon—living in her mother's locket could never terrorize anyone again. She turned away from him, busying herself refilling the shampoo. He usually went away if she ignored him long enough.

He glided to a stop directly in front of her, his amorphous lower body bisected by the rim of the sink. "How about I swap it out for a new wish?"

She shook her head, refusing to look at him.

He slid closer and leered in her face. "You're going to lose the salon."

Her upset stomach tightened into a rock, hating that he was right. Every time she tried to settle into one spot and build a life, something went wrong, and she was certain her demon had a hand in it, much as he denied it. She'd grow comfortable, make a few friends, then somehow everything would get ripped out from under her. If she wasn't going to embrace the fulfillment of her wish, he'd take away anything that might pass as a surrogate.

Most recently, her landlord had raised the rent on her crappy little lease, hoping to edge her out and demolish the aging building to make way for a new hotel. She and a handful of fellow tenants were putting up a good fight, but it wasn't a battle she was likely to win. And finding a lease she could afford elsewhere in town would be next to impossible.

The bell tinkled, this time for real, and the apparition of her demon popped out of existence. "I'll be right with you!" Tanika called, drying her hands on a nearby towel.

Instead of her first client, Mr. Daniels stood at the door, his white apron smudged with what looked like chocolate. "I brought you an éclair, Tanika. Before they're all gone."

"Oh, Mr. Daniels, you didn't have to do that." Her hips were curvy enough without his constant feeding. Not that she was going to say no to a chocolate éclair.

"It's nothing." The white-haired old man took her hand and placed the cream-filled delight in her palm. "I still owe you for cleansing my place of that pesky spirit."

Heat crept up Tanika's throat. The pesky spirit had been her demon, and once she'd figured out he was making trouble after hours, she'd moved her mother's locket off-site to a safe deposit box. Now the djinn could only materialize through the connection of her unspent wish, keeping his power limited to her direct physical vicinity. "You don't owe me anything, Mr. Daniels."

"I tell all my customers about you." He looked around at the shabby interior. "I don't know why you and Birdie can't get more business."

She shrugged. "Not many people believe in magic. Why do you think I'm cutting hair on the side?"

"You don't read the bumps on people's heads?"

Phrenology? Damn. Why hadn't she thought of that? She'd need to add it to her list of services. "Uh, yes. Yes, I do."

He glanced at her wall clock. "I'd better get back to the cafe, my dear. Have a good morning."

Although it was barely after eight a.m., Tanika plopped down in her hairdresser chair and took a big bite of éclair. With no telling what the future might bring, she was going to enjoy every moment of what she had right now.

Ophir laughed as his convertible took the corner with a squeal of rubber. These modern human inventions almost made living on Earth bearable. Almost.

He pulled into a parallel parking spot along the row of run-down storefronts. Whenever he came to a new town, he liked to hit the oldest neighborhoods first, searching out the antique shops for any sign of his kin. Over the centuries, he'd caught whiffs of portals, but always arrived too late to pinpoint the source. After so many failures, his search had become more of a habit than an intent.

Getting out of the car, he paused on the sidewalk, trying to decide which persona to adopt for this mid-America Main Street kind of town. Although he couldn't change his six-foot-three height, bone structure, or skin color, he'd become quite adept at altering his clothing, posture, and voice to affect anything from geeky college student to wealthy billionaire. Today he decided to choose the latter, but in a low-key sort of way, magically fitting himself with a pair of Givenchy jeans and an untucked button down shirt.

The door of the dive cafe he'd parked next to swung open, letting out a waft of fresh baked goods along with a young woman carrying a white paper bag. He smiled at her and she drew up short, her mouth hanging open. He was quite used to this reaction from women, especially in this persona. "This place any good?" he asked.

"Yes," the woman said in a breathy voice.

"Thanks." He winked and moved past her to the door. He'd developed a fondness for sweets, discovering that an infusion of sugary carbs staved off the weakness he experienced being away from his home dimension. If he carb-loaded, he could sometimes even manage the more exhausting spells without being laid out for days afterward. The energy burst was nothing compared to the energy a djinn acquired upon harvesting a soul, but carbs were easier to acquire.

Inside, the cafe's cheery interior surprised him. Buttery yellow walls with white trim made the place seem larger around the three small wood tables. A handwritten sign at the door said WELCOME, PLEASE ORDER AT THE COUNTER. At the back, a large glass case displayed rows upon rows of freshly-baked cookies, breads, and pastries.

Moving past the tables, he stood behind a man in a charcoal-gray suit placing his order. At the register, an old man in a white apron greeted the customer by name and quickly took his order, handing him a cup of coffee to sip while he waited for his food. Ophir stepped up to the counter, eyeing the sumptuous desserts in the case. "What do you recommend?"

The old man's eyes were red-rimmed and tired, but he smiled and pointed to a chocolate-glazed eclair. "I only make these once a week, and they go fast. If you're in the mood for something to stick to your ribs, we're offering free-range turkey club sandwiches today."

"I'll take three eclairs," Ophir dug into his pocket and pulled out his wallet. "And what the heck, a sandwich, too."

"Something to drink?"

"Coffee with ten sugars."

Raising his brows, the old man produced the coffee plus a white bag with the eclairs. "There's sugar over there." He pointed to a small ledge near the exit that held a tall white sugar dispenser and a carafe that presumably held cream. "Sandwich'll be just a minute."

Ophir poured his sugar then took a seat against the wall. The door jingled, and an older woman entered. Her plain cotton-print dress screamed poverty, but she wore antique cameo earrings and paid in coins out of her vintage sequined coin purse. *Stingy widow but spoils her grandkids.* He once would've used his people-reading skills to play on a human's greatest fears or deepest vices, encouraging them to make a wish that would expend their soul. Now he only read people out of curiosity.

Closing his eyes, he tipped his chair back against the wall, breathing the buttery-yeasty-cinnamon-chocolate-vanilla air. Oh, so many delights to sample. He'd have to remember this place while he was here in town. The scent of anise drifted his direction, and he inhaled deeply.

His eyes popped open.

Anise?

The scent lingered around the woman who'd just entered. His chair clattered sideways to the floor as he launched himself at the woman. She took a step back, one hand fluttering to her heart. "Excuse me?" she asked.

His nostrils flared, eyes scouring her from head to toe. The scent was on her, but not *from* her. It trailed toward the door like perfumed breadcrumbs. Spinning, he dashed for the exit, yanking the door open so hard the glass rattled.

"Sir! Your sandwich!"

Ophir didn't bother with a response. On the sidewalk, the trail led to the right. He shoved past a wide-eyed passerby. The scent was fresh and sharp, guiding him as surely as a leash.

He passed a bicycle repair shop, a vacant storefront, a photo shop. The scent ended as suddenly as it began, and he realized he'd overshot. Veering around, he slammed open a blackened glass door and entered a shop curiously devoid of appeal. Two shabby hairdresser chairs sat to the left, their accompanying mirrors hand painted with the names Birdie and Tanika across the tops. A ceiling-to-floor velvet curtain cordoned off an area at the back next to a small door marked "restroom." No one was in sight, but the anise scent filled the place like heat in an oven. It coated everything with an oily magic that would make a mortal's eyes slide away in disinterest. *Interesting spell choice for a place of business.*

Ophir's gaze cut right through the glamour. A portal had been used here for at least a few, solid years to have left behind this thick residue.

From a small door at the back, he heard a toilet flush, then a woman emerged, her dark curls a tangled mess on top of her head. Dark eyes, olive skin, cheeks still rounded by youth. Gypsy ancestry. She wore a billowy blouse that floated over her hips in a feather-light caress but still managed to show off the rounded curves of her breasts. Despite his urgency to find the portal, his cock stirred.

Her face broke into a genuine smile. "Welcome to the Seance Salon! How can I help you?"

"I'm... looking for someone." He shifted his gaze around the room, trying to pinpoint the source of the magic. But the portal had apparently been here so long, opened and closed so often, it was impossible to pick out a single location.

"Oh." Her smile faltered, then resumed in a more plastic fashion. Her voice had lost its perky hopefulness. "I'm afraid I'm the only one here. Perhaps I could interest you in a reading?"

He narrowed his eyes, trying to read her, but the oily magic was causing interference. He'd only encountered a handful of humans with a hint of their own magic during his many centuries on Earth. Most genuine magic came from a human passing off a djinn's powers as their own. She must know about the portal. Perhaps during her "reading" she'd reveal its location. He forced his shoulders to relax and smiled. "I think I'd like that."

She blinked. "You would? I mean... of course! Come this way."

Leading the way, she pushed aside the worn velvet curtain to reveal a table draped in a cheap red tablecloth flanked by two folding chairs. He stepped inside the cramped space, senses alert for any sign of the portal. The curtain dropped behind them, plunging them into semi-darkness, and she moved to the opposite side of the table. A match grated to life, polluting the anise scent with burning sulphur, followed by a candle smelling of bay leaf and vanilla.

He frowned. "Do you have to burn that?"

She paused, flame hovering over a second candle. The flickering light reflected from her eyes. "It helps me center my psychic energies."

Being this close to a portal was making him antsy. If he could touch her, he could at least determine if she had the portal on her. Maybe even cut through the magic to gauge her fears and desires. Clenching his jaw, he thrust a hand across the table. "You read palms?"

She blew out the match and gave him an uncomfortable smile. "I'm afraid I have to ask for payment up front."

He stifled a laugh. Of course she wanted money. She was a gypsy. Who needed magic to read this kind of human? Digging out his wallet, he pulled several hundred dollar bills free and let them flutter to the table. He had no time to haggle. "Enough?"

Her dark eyes went round, and she nodded tightly, sweeping the bills toward her. "What's your name?" she asked.

He thrust out his hand again, laying it palm up on the table. "Ophir."

"Ophir." She rolled the word around on her tongue, and he was surprised to find himself wondering what that tongue might feel like running over his cock. "That's an unusual name. Ancient."

"I know," he growled, trying to stay focused. It had been a long time since a woman had exerted this kind of influence on him. *Find the portal, then you can dally.* He wriggled his fingers insistently.

Without touching him, she leaned over the table to look, her breath tickling his flesh. Above the gaping neckline of her shirt, her cleavage seemed to scream for his attention. She studied his open hand, still without touching. What was she doing? He curled his fingers into a fist, hiding his palm.

She looked up to meet his gaze, her dark eyes like vortexes in the candlelight. "I can't read it if you don't show me."

He swallowed, mouth suddenly and inexplicably dry. "Don't you need to touch me? To trace my lifeline?"

"I prefer not to influence the reading with my own aura."

He flared his nostrils, quickly running out of patience. Slowly he uncurled his fingers, curious what line of bullshit she'd feed him about his future.

She stared down again, her gaze lingering for what felt like an eternity. When she finally looked up, her brows were furrowed. "I'm not... your lines are all there, but they read like a textbook. Like they were drawn on instead of emerging from your soul."

Ophir jerked his hand back as if burned. He looked into her eyes, pulling threads of his magic around him like cloak, unsure if he should run away or move closer. Had he actually found a human who could touch his realm? She'd definitely seen something of the truth, but didn't understand. And he had no idea what that meant.

She chewed one corner of her upper lip, her gaze shifting to her lap. Slowly, she brought the money he'd given her back into view. Shoving the bills across the table at him, she said, "I'm sorry."

He stared at the money, stunned. The paper meant nothing to him. He could conjure more whenever he pleased. What surprised him was that she was giving it back. And very little about humans surprised him these days. Shaking his head, he said, "Tell you what. You let me read your palm, and you can keep the money."

Her gaze cut to him, suspicion flickering in her eyes. "You want to pay me to read my palm? Why?"

He shrugged and held out his hand in request. "Call it a whim."

After a moment, she lay the back of her hand against his open palm. Her face remained completely serious. "Okay. But if this is a gimmick to ask me out, the answer is no. And I'm still keeping the money."

Chuckling, Ophir wrapped his large hand around her smaller one and drew it close. Her knuckles were slightly chapped, but the rest of her skin was soft and warm. A fresh, citrusy smell rose from her flesh, and he breathed deep, seeking the sharp anise bite of djinn magic. It was there, ingrained within her flesh, as if her very cells were infused with the power.

And he still couldn't read her.

He caressed her wrist with his thumb, sensing the very mortal pulse beneath her skin. There was something more within her, something of his own world. Something djinn. Certainly she wasn't the *source* of the magic? A portal had to be metal.

"So what's it say?" she asked, interrupting his thoughts.

Keeping his face serious, he leaned forward over the table. He wasn't sure what was going on here, but he knew how to find out. "Believe it or not, it says you're going to go out with me."

From where the stranger's fingers wrapped around Tanika's wrist, a shiver ran up her arm and seemed to settle in her chest. More unexpectedly, a heated longing began to pulse deep in her core. She got asked out on a regular basis, but always said no. Dating meant emotion. Attachment. A longing for family. The one thing she could never have. To allow such a thing to come true would release her djinn, and she'd sworn to do anything it took to take him to the grave for what he'd done.

At twenty-seven years old, she was still a virgin, and planned to be until the day she died. Yet this man, this strange and sexy man, gave her the urge to break her rule, just this once.

"You don't even know my name," she said, her heart thundering in her ears.

"Mmmm," he said, screwing one coffee-brown eye half-closed and peering at her palm. He had lashes a supermodel would be jealous of. "I'm going to say your name is... Tanika."

She gasped and jerked her hand away, her heartbeat turning from excited to fearful. Her mother'd had the sight much stronger than Tanika, but even she couldn't guess a person's name by looking at their palm. "How on Earth could you see that there?"

He grinned and jerked a thumb over his shoulder. "Normally, a magician doesn't reveal his secrets. But your name is painted across the mirror out there. I took a chance that you don't look like someone called Birdie."

Tanika relaxed into her folding chair. He was just a player. That, she could handle. *Tit for tat.* Reaching out, she retrieved the bills still lying on the table and tucked them into her pocket. With these, she'd be able to stave off eviction for at least another month. Putting on her most mysterious smile, she looked at him through her lashes. "I'm afraid I don't date. But if you'd like to come back for another reading tomorrow after my psychic energies have renewed themselves, I'd be happy to look into your fortune again."

He leaned his broad shoulders back against his chair, folding his hands in his lap, his eyes dancing with mirth. "How do you know I have a fortune?"

Flushing, Tanika put a hand to her neck. "I didn't mean... I was only offering..."

"Oh, now my sweet little gypsy girl's all flustered." The sultry depth of his voice reminded her of a tiger about to pounce, and his perfect white smile threatened to dazzle her. No one man deserved to have so much sex appeal.

"I don't want you to think I'm after your money."

"Well, aren't you?"

She blinked, unsure how to answer. Of course she was after his money. Just not in an underhanded sort of way. "I'll give you your next reading for free."

"I'd much rather you simply went out with me."

"I already said no."

"I believe in second chances."

She licked her lips, wondering what a date with this man might be like. She'd never been on a date. Not once. Although she hadn't been able to read his fortune, she'd had a lot of experience reading people in general. Ophir seemed like the kind of guy who'd treat a girl like a princess, at least for the short duration he was playing her. Plus he was sexy as hell. She shook her head, squeezing her thighs together. Sex wouldn't fulfill her wish, but her djinn would do anything he could to make her wish come true, even turn a player into a devoted husband. Yet... how would it feel to kiss Ophir? To even *say* she'd kissed a man like Ophir?

The bell at the entrance rang, and Birdie's familiar mincing footsteps clicked across the linoleum, bringing Tanika back to reality. She rose and pushed the heavy velvet curtain aside. "I'm sorry. I just can't."

Ophir stood as well, moving closer to her than he needed to exit. His impressive height made her dizzy as much as the masculine scent surrounding him. Was that Polo? He leaned down close to whisper in her ear. "You will. I'm a patient man."

With that, he turned toward Birdie. "You must be Birdie! Perhaps you could find time to give me a trim?"

Tanika watched as the petite woman flushed to her platinum blonde roots while Ophir took a seat in her chair. She shot Tanika a glance as if asking for permission. Tanika shrugged and nodded. Let him move his attention to another woman. No skin off her nose.

Yet as Birdie trimmed his hair, chattering about inane things like the weather, Tanika found herself looking for tasks to keep her nearby, her gaze straying to Ophir's handsome face far too often. And worse, catching him looking back at her—far too often—the sexy hint of a dimple at the edge of his mouth.

Unsurprisingly, he gave Tanika a broad wink, paid in cash, and sauntered out the door without a backward glance.

Birdie collapsed into her chair. She kicked off her high heels and fanned herself with the hundred dollar bill he'd left. "Where'd that hunk of man come from?"

Tanika blinked at the door, still feeling dazed, then returned her attention to the curlers she was sorting for the third time. "He just walked in here off the street. Said he was looking for someone."

"Lordy, he can look for someone in my seat any time he likes. Or under my seat, if you know what I mean." Birdie sat up and tucked the bill into her bra. "Why didn't he ask you to trim his hair?"

Shrugging, Tanika carried the curlers back to the plastic storage shelf. "Spreading the wealth? I gave him a reading. Or tried."

"What do you mean?"

She shook her head, remembering the strange, rubbery resistance when she'd focused her sight on him. "It was weird. Like he'd been coated in plastic or something. I could see the surface, but not the real man underneath."

"Ohhh, mysterious. Maybe now someone'll finally pique your interest, eh?"

Tanika snorted. "Yeah, right. Like he'd be interested in me."

"The way he kept looking at you in the mirror, I don't think he heard a word I said."

"No one hears a word you say, Birdie. You talk about the weather."

"What'm I supposed to talk about?"

"I don't know. Juicy stuff."

Birdie hopped out of the chair and grabbed the broom, sweeping up the nearly non-existent traces of Ophir's hair. "Not all of us have the sight to find the juicy stuff."

Tanika placed a hand over her heart. "I never use my gift for evil."

"Mmm. Well, maybe you should once in a while. At least to get us more customers like that."

Sighing, Tanika went to fetch the dustpan. Any more customers like that, and her demon might just get his wish.

*O*phir returned to the bakery to find the eclairs sold out. Disappointed, he bought a huge blueberry muffin and three cookies instead and sat at one of the tables, watching customers come and go in the small cafe. Over the centuries, he'd gone through periods of indulgence—food, drink, sex, even some of the interesting drugs created by humans. His immortal body could be drowned in pleasures the same way a mortals could. But unlike mortals, a saturation of vice always ended in boredom rather than death.

The luscious gypsy was an interesting conundrum. A way home, or something else? Perhaps she carried a whisper of djinn blood. It would explain the tingle of magic rising from her skin. His blood heated at the thought of her skin. *All* her skin, naked, lounging on a bed of silk pillows, her glossy black hair spread like a fan around her head. How long had it been since a mortal had intrigued him? He hadn't allowed himself to become interested, let alone attached, to one of the short-lived creatures since Emelda had been taken from him.

A raw spot deep inside him threatened to open again, and he shook his head to clear it. No time to fall into that pit now. A portal was nearby. Home was nearby, full of fellow djinn with lives long enough to matter. No more living among these painfully short-lived humans. He only had to figure out how to convince Tanika to open up.

Licking crumbs from his fingers and sipping his coffee, he watched a small boy press his forehead against the cafe's display case while his mother paid for their order. Mortals. They were made to die; the young were especially vulnerable. Yet somehow the race pressed on as if they were doing something that mattered. He'd watched generation after generation refuse to learn from previous mistakes.

Well, he'd learned from his. No getting attached to mortals.

Tanika was mortal, therefore his only interest in her must remain only a means to an end. Like any mortal with access to a djinn, she'd keep that knowledge close. He'd need to seduce it out of her. But she'd already made it very clear she wasn't interested. She'd stood firm against him, his money, even his subtle come-hither magic. At first he'd thought it was the glamour magic he'd detected throughout the salon interfering, but Birdie had reacted as expected. Only Tanika was immune. He'd have to seduce the sexy gypsy the hard way, with charm.

The cafe owner approached Ophir's table with a pot of coffee in one hand. Flour dusting his forearms, walking with the care of someone on sore feet, but Ophir sensed the fellow loved his shop, loved the community he felt it built. "Refill?" the man asked.

Ophir nodded and slid his cup forward. This persona was by far one of his favorites. Both women and men responded favorably to a tall, handsome, and obviously rich man in his prime. "Thank you."

The man poured steaming, fragrant coffee into the cup. "I haven't seen you here before. You new in town?"

"I am. The name's Ophir." He held out a hand to shake. "You seem to get a lot of regulars in here."

"Only way I'm keeping the doors open. Gregory Daniels."

"Seems to be tough times around here." Ophir exhaled a small trust spell at the old man, hoping to glean more information. "You know Tanika? At the salon?"

The wrinkles in Mr. Daniels's face creased into a smile. "You a friend of Tanika?"

"Just met her, actually. I'd like to ask her out."

"Oh, she's a gem. Works way too hard. Here." Daniels retreated behind the counter and emerged with a small bag. "Take this to her. She has a soft spot for sweets." He winked.

Soft spot for sweets. Good to know. Ophir bowed his head gratefully. "You're too kind."

"Be good to her. She doesn't go out much."

"I'll do my best." Ophir dropped a hundred dollar bill on the table, and headed for the door, thinking of just how good he'd like to be to her.

On the sidewalk, the late afternoon sunlight reflected off the pavement while the rumble of passing cars filled the air. A homeless man sat with his legs stretched across half the sidewalk, calling after a woman who scurried past. "Marry me! Marry me!"

Flicking out a spell to encourage the man to sleep, Ophir stepped around him. No wonder these businesses were struggling. He headed to the salon, breathing deeply of anise. Inside, Birdie hovered over an elderly lady in her chair. She looked over her shoulder toward the door. "Why, hello, again!"

Scanning the small area, Ophir held up the small bag. "I have a delivery for Tanika."

"Oh, no! She just left." Birdie's brows scrunched into genuine regret, and he found himself liking her despite himself. She licked her lips and glanced at the wall clock. "I don't think she's coming back tonight."

Ophir opened the bag and looked inside. A glossy chocolate eclair lay cradled in frilly paper at the bottom. He chuckled. "That old baker told me he'd sold out."

"You mean Mr. Daniels?"

"I understand Tanika enjoys pastry." Ophir cocked his head. He might as well begin practicing coercion without using magic. "Any way you can let her know I'm here?"

Birdie grinned. "Atta boy. Why don't I call her? You can wait if you like."

"I would much appreciate it."

While she hurriedly dug out her phone and dialed, he strolled back to the curtained area. Might as well use this time to search for the portal. Leaving a djinn talisman unattended would be a novice mistake, but then, Tanika *was* human. Her race had been making novice mistakes for millennia.

He ran his fingertips down the velvet curtain, across the rickety table, and to the chair where Tanika had sat. The entire salon stank of hair chemicals and scented candles, but beneath it lay the remnants of magic, both old and new. Glancing toward Birdie, who was talking into her phone and looking at him through her lashes, he nonchalantly sat in the psychic's chair and ran a hand beneath the table. Nothing there. He set the bag down and let his gaze roam the walls. A cheap plastic clock shaped like a cat and an old framed photo were the only decorations besides mirrors. Rising, he moved to the photo, bending slightly to look at the weathered faces of two women glaring back at him as if they hadn't wanted a picture taken. Their dark curly hair reminded him of Tanika. Relatives?

Birdie called across the salon, "She'll be here in a few minutes."

Moving to Tanika's chair, he sniffed for magic while he lowered himself onto the worn pleather. Still nothing. The old lady in Birdie's chair beamed at him. "Aren't you a strapping young man?"

He smiled politely, itching to search the counter and mirror. He could have cast a shielding spell to allow him to do just that, but for some reason the idea of going about charming Tanika without magic had a strong hold on him, and he wanted to "play fair," if only in his mind. Instead of using magic, he sat and stared at each item as if it might start speaking and reveal all the salon's secrets, and hopefully some of Tanika's. Several envelopes sat on the counter, the topmost one stamped with a big, red OVERDUE notice. Cans of hair spray and mousse. Several plastic combs and brushes. Along the left edge of the mirror, photos of random, smiling people overlapped each other in a collage he didn't understand. Nothing old. Nothing metal. Nothing *portal.*

After a few minutes, the bell over the door jingled, and Tanika entered, face slightly flushed and full breasts heaving. Her brows were knit with concern, but the moment her gaze met his in the mirror, she seemed to relax. She glared at Birdie. "You said I had an emergency client."

"This guy's hot enough to set of the smoke alarm." Birdie waved her scissors without looking up. "I call that an emergency."

The lady in her chair covered her laugh with her fingers.

Ophir rose, languidly stretching knowing the effect his body had on most women. "It's an emergency eclair, actually. Mr. Daniels sent it for you. It's the last one, and I'd hate to let it go stale overnight."

Her face softened. "Mr. Daniels? I see. Well, thank you."

"He said you'd split it with me."

She raised one eyebrow at him, a tiny smile toying with the corner of her mouth. "I don't split my desserts. Can't you tell?"

Ophir let out a melodramatic sigh. "Well, then I guess I'll have to eat the rest of it."

"The rest of it?"

He shrugged. "I was hungry."

"You ate my eclair?" She blinked at him, as if she truly couldn't believe his words.

He smiled his best, sexiest smile. It'd been eons since he'd had to rely purely on wits and charm, and he felt a little rusty. The challenge was delicious, especially with someone as stubborn as Tanika. "Let me make it up to you with dinner."

She crossed her arms, face hardening. "I said I'm not going out with you."

"Give me one good reason why not."

Birdie spoke up behind him. "She doesn't date."

Tanika glowered in her direction.

Perhaps a previous heartbreak had made her wary? He took a breath and changed tactics. "I'm not asking for a date. I'm repaying you for the eclair."

The old lady's wavering voice chimed in. "Give the fellow a chance."

"Surely you eat dinner?" Ophir asked.

"I said no," Tanika gritted between her teeth.

The woman was more than a challenge. She was impossible. How could he charm her without magic? He recalled the overdue bills on the counter. Perhaps he could find another way to engage her. He let out a melodramatic sigh. "I'd hoped to be more subtle about this, but I guess I'll get right to the point. I want to invest in your salon."

The room went silent, even the snip snip of Birdie's scissors going still.

"Do you think I'm stupid?" Tanika asked. "Nobody would want to invest in this place."

He held up both hands, palms out. He'd finally hit a nerve. But he'd have to play this carefully or she'd toss him out on his ear. "You're the first genuine psychic I've met. An honest to God human being with a hint of real magic," he said. The truth of his words stirred his blood. If he never found a portal home, she might be the closest thing to his kind he'd ever find. He moved forward and put a hand on her elbow. The soft skin beneath his fingertips sent an unexpected thrill of pleasure up his arm. "Can we talk about it over dinner?"

For a brief moment, she resisted the pressure of his hand.

He curled his fingers around her inner arm, stroking his middle finger over the tender crease inside the bend. A tiny shiver rippled across her skin beneath his fingertips, and a flush infused her cheeks. He smiled and in a low, intimate voice, asked, "Please?"

To his delight, she allowed him to guide her to his convertible.

4

anika fastened her seatbelt, still in a daze as she watched Ophir round the front of the bright red Ferrari convertible to get into the driver's seat. *Holy shit, he drives a fucking Ferrari.* If she hadn't already been under some sort of hormonal haze from his touch on her arm, she's have been swooning in her seat. From the moment he'd first walked in the salon door, she'd been having X-rated fantasies, and now she was on a date with him. In a Ferrari. Or the closest thing to a date she'd ever have.

It's only a business dinner, she reminded herself. But she couldn't keep her eyes off the broad cut of his shoulders or the way his ass looked in those undoubtedly expensive jeans.

He slid into the seat and looked over at her. "Top down?"

All she could think about was flashing him her breasts. Her nipples hardened at the thought of his gaze lingering over her flesh. Fingers brushing the sensitive rosy tips. Maybe that sensual mouth of his...

She jerked back to reality and nodded, highly conscious of his masculine cologne from where she sat. He started the engine. In mute fascination, she watched his hand move to the gear stick, ease the car into first. So close to her left knee it sent a shiver of pleasure up her leg, pooling low and hot in her belly. She fought the urge to open her knees and make contact with that hand. She was a virgin, but that didn't mean she couldn't imagine what it might feel like to let his palm move over and slide up her inner thigh...

Jerking her gaze away, she squeezed her knees together and forced herself to stare out the windshield.

He pulled into traffic and quickly sped up, taking them sharply around a corner and shooting for the ramp to the freeway.

Her stomach quivered at the acceleration. He darted around a lumbering box truck, sailing past a line of traffic on the right. She grinned, her curls whipping about her face.

He glanced at her. "You like speed?"

"Oh, yes," she gasped, throwing her head back as the car surged forward. Speed was delicious.

He shifted gears again, sliding between two sedans before easing into the slow lane. Then they throttled up again, the convertible's engine throbbing deep in her bones.

All too soon, they reached the exit, and he slowed to a more reasonable pace for the side streets. They glided to a stop outside Bottega Soleil, the fanciest French restaurant in town. The place was supposedly booked solid months in advance. Hadn't he said he was new in town?

She pushed her hair out of her face with both hands, breathless from his seduction of speed, and reached for the door handle. He already had the door open for her, a hand extended to help her rise from the low seat. How'd he done that? This was beginning to feel more and more like a date. Perspiration prickled beneath her arms. She accepted his offered hand, her skin tingling at the contact, and rose from the bucket seat. "You know you can't get in here without a reservation?"

"Don't worry." He smirked. "I'll get us a table."

He cupped her elbow, making her heart race, and guided her to the door. The maître d looked up and smiled at them—well, at Ophir. His disdainful gaze swept over Tanika's cheap black slacks and peasant blouse and refused to look again.

"Wait here," Ophir said, and sauntered toward the man. After a few short words and a generous tip, the man ushered them back into the subtly lit dining area. A string quartet played softly in one corner of the room, and burgundy tablecloths fell in perfect pleats from all the tables, each place setting gleaming with crystal and silver. Single white rosebuds served as centerpieces, and the guests wore pearls and ties. To her surprise, the maître d held her chair back for her, shook her napkin and placed it on her lap.

"Thank you," she murmured.

The waitress arrived on the maître d's heels, setting a basket on the table and handing them each a menu. She smiled brightly at Ophir, fingers toying with the top button of her blouse as she handed him a wine list. "May I start you off with a drink?"

Ophir took the list without looking at the woman, his gaze solidly on Tanika. "Do you prefer red or white?"

Tanika's skin tingled under his attention, pooling deep in her core. Never in her life had she experienced a reaction like this to a man. Everything he did seemed to have a sexual connotation, albeit only in her own mind. He made her... giddy. There was no other way to describe it. Shaking her head, she folded her hands in her lap. "Water's fine." Best to keep a straight head around this guy.

Ophir handed the list back. "We'll start with fresh fruit and cheese, plus two glasses of house red."

The waitress bobbed her head and sauntered off. Tanika remained ramrod straight in her chair, her gaze on Ophir. "Let's keep this professional."

He lifted his napkin between two manicured fingers and flicked it open before laying it across his lap. "How am I not professional?"

"You ordered wine."

"You've never had wine at a business dinner?" He raised a brow.

Tanika suddenly felt three inches tall. "I've actually never been on a business dinner."

A sexy smile caressed his mouth. "*I've* never met such an honest gypsy."

Her chest tightened. Her mother'd called herself a gypsy. Tanika's first eight years of life had been spent on the road. Her wish for a husband and family had arisen out of a desire for stability. Hands bunching into fists in her lap, Tanika replied with a whisper she wasn't even sure Ophir could hear. "I'm not a gypsy."

He cocked his head, as if listening to something deeper than her words. "I suppose you're not, at that."

The waitress returned with two glasses of wine and

left. The string quartet began to play a familiar waltz, each note thrumming the air like a heartbeat. Ophir picked up his wine glass and sipped, his deep brown eyes regarding her over the glass. Uncomfortable, she stared at her own glass, but didn't touch it. "Why did you bring me here, really?" she asked.

A moment passed. "I really do want to invest in you. You see the future?"

Taking a breath, she thought about how to put her gift into words. "Not so much the future. More like... a person's desire."

"And you exploit that."

"No!" Her mother had used her sight that way. Gauged a client's deepest desire, and then loosed the djinn on those most willing to pay. The client would get their wish, Mom would get her money, and the demon would gain another soul. "I never use my gift to exploit. Only empower."

"Well, there's your problem. You undersell yourself. Sounds like you need a business advisor."

She looked away. Birdie always asked her the same thing. The truth was, she didn't charge enough. Sometimes she gave out advice for free. Her clients were often lower-income, and needed a shoulder to cry on as much as anything. How did this stranger know so much about her? "My clients don't have a lot of money."

"I assume most of them wish for wealth. Can't you... guide them... toward that?"

"Most people say they want money, but if you look deeper, you'll find they actually want something else. Something they think money can buy them. Usually it can't. I help them focus on the things they want that are right in front of them."

A small platter of cheeses, grapes, figs, and melon seemed to appear on the table before them, almost as if by magic. Ophir selected a plump grape, popped it into his mouth, and chewed slowly. Did every move he made have to be so damn sexy?

"And besides." Tanika reached for a bite of melon, inhaling the sweet, dewy scent before nibbling on it. "If I knew how to get my hands on a load of cash, don't you think I would have by now?"

He laughed. "I thought that's why you're talking to me?"

Tanika smiled, refusing to take his bait. "You're the one who insisted on taking me to dinner. Are you saying you're my wish come true?"

"I can be if you'd like me to be." The low rumble of his voice and the intensity of his gaze made her insides quiver.

She looked away, studying the other guests while she regained her composure. Nearly all couples. One family in the corner had a small child. Who could afford to bring a child to a restaurant like this? Another couple nearby sat looking deeply into one another's eyes, the wife's pregnant belly pressed into the lip of the table. She couldn't hide the bitterness in her voice as she said, "You have no idea what my wish is."

The waitress appeared again, and Tanika realized she hadn't even opened the menu. Without batting an eye, Ophir ordered for both of them, and the waitress whisked the menu boards away. "I'm fairly good at guessing a woman's desires," he said, his voice sultry. She sucked in a sharp breath as he leaned forward. "Give me your hand."

Without thinking, she offered him her palm, assuming he was going to play at reading her again. His long fingers wrapped gently around hers and he rose from the table, pulling her to her feet. "May I have this dance?"

Without giving her time to respond, he pulled her toward the quartet. A small dance floor sat between the players and the tables, but no one used it. She spluttered, hyper aware of every eye in the restaurant following them. Her pulse in her ears drowned out the string quartet's song. "I don't know—"

At the edge of the parquet, he swiveled, pulling her to him with one fluid twitch of his muscular arm. She found herself pressed against his chest, his hands at her waist, his feet guiding her as if they'd been performing together for years. Up close, his masculine scent made her mouth water.

She smoothed her trembling fingers up the hard planes of his chest to settle on his shoulders, allowing herself to be swept along. The watching restaurant guests faded to meaninglessness. This moment was exactly what she'd always dreamed her prom would be. Or her wedding dance. She tilted her face up to look at him. Dark stubble dusted his angular jawline, and the ring of lashes around his eyes almost made her think he had to be wearing makeup. What would it be like, to have just one night with a man like this? Even one kiss?

He smiled down at her. "You look lovely when you blush."

The heat that had crept across her face during the walk to the dance floor intensified at his words. But she didn't let go. She hadn't had a drop to drink, and yet there it was, the dizzy, giddy swimming sensation of being swept off her feet. "Do people dance together at business dinners?"

His lips grazed her ear, and his low voice shot straight to her core, melting her knees. "If they don't, they should, don't you think?"

He squeezed her tightly against him, spinning a

small circle that left her even more lightheaded. Her body thrummed with desire from her scalp to her toes. She clung to him as he settled into a steady rhythm that had her thinking of other rhythms she'd never experienced. Oh, God, was that his hard on she felt pressed against her? The heat of it threatened to burn her clothes right off her body.

Closing her eyes, she turned her face toward him, the scrape of his stubble along her cheek as thrilling as any car ride. She'd never been this close to a man. Probably never would again. A small voice inside her urged her on. One kiss, just to try it. They were in a public place, so what could go wrong? His breath fanned against her, flaming her passion higher.

Then his lips met hers in a blaze of light.

5

Ophir had intended the kiss to be quick, almost chaste. A test of her desire. Instead, he found himself devouring her lips, every atom of his being striving to join hers as his tongue explored her mouth. His pulse kicked up when she moaned, soft and thrumming, melting into his arms as if she, too, felt the need to entwine their souls. He matched her growing passion. It was impossible not to. A slow burn spread through him the longer they kissed, still rocking in time to the string quartet, and he fed the fire with each rolling thrust of his tongue. He'd never felt so hungry. So crazed with lust. Desire hooked into every thread of his being with a force as intoxicating as if he'd claimed her human soul.

Yet here she stood, alive and well, her lush body

aligned with his, nipples hard against his chest. Her fingers dug into his shoulders, pulling him closer, as if she were afraid he was going to disappear.

He had no intention of disappearing.

Tilting his hips, he pressed his rock-hard cock against the softness of her belly. A rippling shudder rolled through her, and he gripped her hips firmly. Her passion was more than a drug. It was like magic. He craved more.

She pulled back with a gasp, breaking the contact of their lips. "I don't think this is a good idea."

He leaned closer, brushing his lips against her cheek. "You taste of magic, Tanika. I wish for more."

She exhaled a waft of anise-sweet breath against his neck and tilted her face away, exposing her neck. "We can't always have what we wish for."

Rather than taking it as a rebuff, he took it as an invitation, and lowered his face to the crook of her throat, brushing his nose along her satiny skin. He opened his lips slightly and took a deep breath, tasting her pheromones along with the magic. Great Allah, he wanted her. Wanted to pour his energy within her. To see what might come of a union with this mortal. The desire shocked him.

He pulled away to look into her eyes. Not even Emelda, with her harem training, had ignited within him a lust this primal, a desire to become one. Tanika was an intriguing blend of innocence and worldliness he'd never before encountered. And the sweet anise scent of her skin spoke of more than mortal blood. Yes, of course. That was the driver for his intense reaction. After so long away from his own kind, the magic coursing through her blood was triggering his instincts. His cock throbbed painfully and his balls felt weighted with iron as he thought of claiming her. Portal be damned, he needed this woman.

He slid a hand up her back to cup the nape of her neck. "Sometimes wishes change."

Her brows scrunched. "Not mine."

"Tell me what you wish for."

"It doesn't matter. Especially to a man like you."

A man like me. How did she see him, exactly? Narrowing his eyes, he cast an obscuring spell about them and pulled her off the dance floor toward the kitchens. Waiters moved out of the way without even realizing, and soon he had her past the cooks and dishwashers to a narrow hall leading to a small, dimly lit manager's office.

She'd followed him dazedly until this moment. At the office door, she pulled back. "I'm not going in there with you."

"Why not?"

"I barely know you. And I'm not the kind of girl who does it in back alleys with strange men. We should go back to the table and talk about the salon." She attempted to duck under his arm and retreat to the bustling kitchen, but he planted his palm against the wall to block her passage. The idea of doing it in a back alley with her—doing it anywhere with her, everywhere with her—raised the flames of his desire to new heights.

"This isn't a back alley," he breathed against her ear, her scent making his mouth water. He was close enough to taste her skin. He resisted. "And we're not done. Not yet. You need to answer my question."

"Which question?"

"About me granting your wish."

She turned squarely to face him and placed her hands on her hips. "Like I haven't heard that line before."

He grinned, feeling very mortal. Vulnerable, even. For some reason it felt good. "Did it work?"

Standing on tiptoes, she pressed her mouth to his ear. "No." She dropped to her normal height. "Our food's probably getting cold."

Instead of moving aside, he grasped her hips and backed her against the wall. His mouth muffled her gasp as he plunged his tongue between her lips, kissing her with deep, rolling thrusts. His hands molded to her waist, but he kept a breath of distance between their bodies, letting her know if she struggled, he'd back off.

She didn't.

To his satisfaction, she grew pliant and leaned into him. Threading her fingers into the curls at the back of his neck, she returned his explorative kisses. Her essence filled him, melded with his magic. Widening his stance, he steadied his legs and thrust a thigh between her legs, pressing her more firmly against the wall. She tilted her hips against him, the heat radiating from between her legs threatening to burn through his pant leg.

As their tongues danced and rolled, the urge to have her grew stronger. Her tiny moans of pleasure acted like quicksand—to resist or struggle would only sink him faster. Every inch of his skin tingled with desire to feel her naked against him.

He shoved the edge of her peasant blouse upward, skimming the satin-soft skin beneath with his palm. *More.* He needed more. Sliding his hand around to her lower back, he dipped inside the waistband of her leggings to cup her ass over her cotton panties. He lifted her against him, kneading her flesh.

She gasped, legs rising to hook around his waist, ankles crossed at his lower back. Damn, she was sexy.

Pulling her off the wall, he carried her inside the office, kicking the door closed behind them. No one would bother them with his spell in place. In the back of his mind, he knew he was making a mistake. The woman kissed him as if she were starving. As if she was a djinn herself, about to consume his soul. The unknowns of her nature chilled him. And yet Tanika was the first female he'd met who stirred his elemental nature. More than just sex, she aroused the pure, raw instincts that drove a djinn to mate.

Mate? The idea frightened as much as drew him. Djinn did not take a mate lightly. Sex was simply release. Mating was binding, as dangerously unbreakable as the magic to grant wishes. And she'd burn out in the blink of an eye.

Don't think about mating. You just need to have her to get her out of your system. Then you can move on.

He carried her to a leather sofa against one wall, wanting to savor her. To make her feel the same intensity of desire he now had coursing through his bloodstream. Lowering her to the cushions without breaking the kiss, he knotted one hand in the curls of hair behind her head to cradle her descent. He settled against her, kissing her deeply, on and on until her legs parted and she looped her free leg behind his knee. His hips settled against her, his throbbing cock pressed hard against her sex. She whimpered, her hands clawing at him, pulling him closer into the kiss as her hips tilted upward against him.

Breaking the kiss, he trailed his mouth along her jaw to nibble at her ear. A shudder ran through her body at the sensitive touch. He slid one hand down over her leggings to caress her inner thigh from knee to groin, thumb pointing a line straight to the apex of his desire.

"What're you doing?" She tightened her grip on his shirt, balling the material in her fists, but she didn't push him away.

"Touching you."

He waited a moment, giving her a chance to deny him, then inched his hand higher, cupping her cloth-covered sex. Heat and dampness met him.

He groaned. The instinct to rip her clothing from her body and plunge himself deep inside her gripped him. She'd fit him perfectly, he could sense it. His cock jerked, taking on a life of its own, and pre-come dampened his boxers. How easy it would be to lose himself in her. He needed to possess her, and nothing was going to stop him.

Propping himself on an elbow, he gazed down at her. It would be too easy to go too fast, to take without concern for her needs, and he wanted her to need him as much as he needed her. Her half-lidded gaze was drowsy on him, her lovely mouth swollen from his kisses. "You enjoy being touched, don't you?"

She swallowed hard, but didn't respond. And he so needed to hear her voice.

"Answer me."

"Yes," she whispered, closing her eyes.

He slid his hand up to her waistband and once again tunneled his fingers beneath the fabric. Easing his fingers under the waistband of her panties, he threaded through the soft curls covering her mound. She sucked in a breath.

Great Allah, he wanted inside. To feel her heat wrapped around him. The excited yet hesitant way her hands clutched his shirt while her stomach trembled made him wonder exactly how experienced she was. From the way she'd kissed, he would've said she'd been around the block. Maybe he'd guessed wrong?

He slipped his fingers deeper, splitting her open. She cried out, buttocks tightening in response to his touch.

"You're wet, Tanika." He stroked the swollen nub of her clit with his middle finger, letting his other two fingers massage her outer lips. "So wet. I like that."

"I shouldn't..." Her bottom squeezed tighter, lifting her toward his touch. "Oh, God. We shouldn't be doing this."

He curled his finger through her folds, probing her opening. "Do you want me to stop?"

"I should say yes." She met his gaze, her irises open windows to her lust. Her upper lip was clamped between her teeth while she panted, telling him of her conflicted desire.

"I won't do anything you don't want me to do." But he didn't give her a chance to reconsider. He tugged her pants down around her hips, exposing her tawny olive skin to his gaze. "I only want to give you pleasure."

"We barely know each other."

At this moment, he was ready to bare his soul to her. Reveal his nature. Grant her every wish. He lowered his face to kiss her exposed hip bone. "We will. I promise you."

She panted, her belly trembling beneath his cheek. "We're in a public place."

"That's why we came back here." He flicked his tongue against her skin, sliding his fingers along her slick folds.

"You planned this?" She panted.

"Not exactly." Teasing her opening, he slid one finger into her tight, wet heat.

She let out a shuddering cry, her velvet core convulsing around him. "Oh, God, that's good."

He pressed a second finger to her opening, and met physical resistance. *She's a virgin?* He nearly lost his rhythm. The knowledge shocked him and raised a protective feeling inside him he hadn't felt for centuries. A need to cherish and nurture. To honor her. Since Emelda, he'd avoided those kinds of feelings at all costs. But now he didn't think that was possible. Tanika was... special.

Continuing to use only one finger, he gently stroked her quivering inner ridges, massaging her clit with his thumb. This woman was becoming more and more intriguing. More and more *his*. "I'm going to make you come until you can think of nothing else."

She let out a throaty groan, and he grinned, dipping his face between her legs and clamping his mouth around her clit while his finger continued stroking. Her flavor flooded him, sweet, salty, and tinged with magic. He thrust inside her as deeply as her tightness allowed, adjusting the speed and angle of his penetration to match her quivering desire.

When he thought she was ready, he masterfully eased another finger inside her, stretching her until she stiffened. Then he curled his tongue around her clit until she bucked against him for more. Again and again, he eased her open, until both fingers pumped in and out of her. Her arousal soaked his hand, and her quickened breathing pressed her pointed nipples against the thin fabric of her blouse. He thrust and licked until her legs were quivering.

"Ophir, please." She rocked against his hand, words full of desperation and need.

He slid his free hand under her bottom, lifting her toward him, and buried his face in her short, wet curls. The fingers pumping into her hooked to reach her G spot, which he'd avoided until now, wanting to bring her as high as possible before sending her over the edge.

This woman was his. Every atom of her, inside and out, belonged to him. When the slight change in the muscles of her core told him it was time, he clamped his mouth over her clit and sucked.

Her body convulsed, her pussy tightening around his fingers with excruciating ecstasy. She cried his name as he tasted her release.

Once she sagged against the cushions, he crawled up and took her mouth in a deep kiss. She sighed, tickling her fingertips along his ribcage to settle on his lower back, pulling him closer.

Such a simple move. And yet it bound him as completely as any portal ever could. A tiny voice in the back of his mind screamed at him to run away, even as a sense of rightness settled over him, like he'd finally come home. He wanted to curl himself around her and hold her for all eternity.

He warred with memories of the last eight hundred years, all the mortals he'd seen come and go. No matter how long they walked the earth, humans eventually passed on. They could be injured. Got sick. Grew old and died. One moment they could be alive and healthy. The next, gone.

And there was a damn good chance he'd just become addicted to this mortal.

anika felt as boneless as a jellyfish, eyes heavy with sleep. She would have succumbed if it hadn't been for the weight of the man lying atop her. His breath heated the curve of her neck while his fingertips skimmed the edge of her breast through her blouse. Her body was too tired to react. Or protest. If he'd wanted to take her right then she wouldn't have objected.

"Why didn't you tell me you're a virgin?" Ophir's voice rumbled close to her ear.

She stiffened, reality crashing down and stealing her breath. *What am I doing?* She shoved against his chest. "Get up."

He lifted himself free and sat back on his heels. She disentangled herself and rolled off the sofa, crawling a few feet away before getting to her feet. Her legs were like rubber bands. *It's only a one time thing. Nothing can come of this.* But her heart ached with the enormity of what had just happened. She wasn't the kind of girl who could treat a heated make-out session like it was a leisure activity. That's why she'd avoided this kind of connection so long. Already she could feel the heartbreaking constriction in her chest at the thought that this man—this gorgeous, thoughtful, sexy-as-hell man—could never be a part of her life.

Scanning the floor for her leggings, she spotted them on the back of the sofa behind Ophir. Rather than brave being near him again, she held out one hand. "Please hand me my clothes."

Without taking his gaze off her, he reached behind him and retrieved the clothing. "Why are you afraid?"

She swallowed, heart thundering against her ribcage. Her muscles ached as if she'd just finished a marathon, and a surprisingly delicious burning between her legs served as a reminder of the heights she'd just reached. Grabbing her pants, she met his gaze. The connection between them pulled her toward him as if only he could alleviate the trembling deep inside her. A longing for passion, affection, and partnership. He made her want to tell the truth. She jerked her gaze away, stepping into her panties. "You'd never believe me."

He swung his legs around to face her, settling his backside into the sofa as if he was about to watch a football game. Except the only entertainment was her struggling back into her clothing. He said, "Try me."

Her stomach dropped. Back at the salon, he'd said he believed in magic. That's what had started this entire thing. Could she confide in him? Would it ruin her chance to save the salon? Or worse, drive him away? This man had just chosen to pleasure her while taking none for himself. The thought of never seeing him again hurt. Settling her waistband around her hips, she took a deep breath and faced him. "Did you really mean it when you said you believe in magic?"

"I do."

"And that's why you want to invest in the salon?"

"Yes."

She pointed a finger back and forth between them. "This can't happen again."

"I can't promise that." The hungry gleam in his eyes made her swallow down her own lust and longing.

"It'd only end in trouble. Believe me."

"How do you know?"

She clenched her teeth. "Because I do."

"Convince me."

Standing there glaring at him, she was torn. The need to justify herself had never felt so strong. *If I tell him, what's the worst that could happen?* He'd think she was crazy and run away forever. Which would probably be a good thing, even if it meant losing his business backing. Still aware they were in a public place but needing to finish this conversation for good, she moved around the desk. She needed something physical in between them to carry on. She'd never talked about her wish with anyone. She wasn't sure why she wanted to now. But Ophir seemed more genuinely interested than anyone she'd ever met. She stared at the stacks of receipts littering the desk, only half-seeing. "My mother and grandmother died when I was eight." She twisted her fingers tightly together, trying to keep the horror that haunted her dreams under control. "They gave their lives for me."

She glanced up, and his attention threatened to burn a hole straight through her. He asked, "That's their photo in the salon?"

She nodded, neck stiff. "It's one of the few things that survived the blast. Besides myself. I survived without a scratch." Her skin prickled with remembered heat, and her blouse stuck to her skin uncomfortably. "The official report said our motor home's propane tank was leaking. But..." She looked at him through her lashes, bracing herself for disbelief and ridicule like she'd received as a child. "The real cause of the explosion was our demon."

He narrowed his eyes. "Demon."

It wasn't a question. It was a statement. What was he thinking? Was he afraid? Did he think she was batshit crazy? Her pulse thrummed in her ears. "I know I sound crazy, but he's real. And you don't need to worry. He's not dangerous. Not anymore."

The demon had taunted her during her early years, telling her to grow up fast so he could be free of the obligation tying him to her. Apparently he hadn't realized her unfulfilled wish would block his greater powers. That he wouldn't be free to harvest more humans until her wish was complete and she was settled in with a loving husband and family. By her eighteenth birthday, when the wish could be granted, she'd resolved to reject it.

Ophir asked, "Is he... still with you?"

Her hand automatically went to her chest, where the pendant had hung for years until she'd discovered the dampening power of the safe deposit box. Ophir's gaze followed her move, then returned to meet her eyes. She chewed her lip, uncomfortable under the scrutiny. "He's restricted to minor magic until he fulfills my wish." She tried to lighten the mood. "I call him a poltergeist, but he hates that."

"I'll bet he does. He probably doesn't like to be called a demon, either." Was that amusement dancing in his eyes? He relaxed back onto the sofa. "So let me get this straight. You made a wish, and you believe your mother and grandmother paid for it?"

"I'd already made the wish when my mom found me, and a wish can't be broken. But it can be renegotiated, so she and Grandma bargained their two souls for my one. I watched them make the deal."

"I'm sorry." His brows drew together in what seemed to be genuine regret. "What did you wish for?"

She swallowed, wondering how he was taking this all in stride, but on the other hand she was glad he wasn't making telling it any harder. Especially now that they were at the point of this confession—the reason she couldn't be with him. Couldn't allow herself to fall for him, not even a little. "To have a loving husband and family and live happily ever after."

He cocked one eyebrow. "Ah, a delayed wish. That makes more sense. You no longer want the wish?"

Tears burned the back of her eyes and she set her jaw, the longing ache within her stronger than she'd ever experienced. "I don't deserve it. It's my responsibility to make sure he never hurts another human being again. If I allow him to fulfill the wish, he's free. If I die before then, he dies with me." She grit her teeth, helpless anger welling up within her. "I'll destroy that evil creature if it's the last thing I do."

"I see." He rose suddenly, his eyes impossible to read. "We'd better get back to our table. I don't know about you, but I'm starving. And we have a business deal to conclude."

Her heartbeat was painful inside her chest. He had no more questions? She hadn't known what she expected, but complete acceptance of her situation—indifference, even—wasn't it. She'd told him she had a demon, for God's sake!

He waited by the door, then escorted her from the office, one hand familiarly on her lower back. Tingles ran up and down her spine at the contact, but he seemed unaware of his effect. The kitchen staff went on about their business, oblivious to their passage, and she wondered if he'd paid them all off. Planned this entire thing. But if that were true, why hadn't he taken full advantage of her? She stumbled back into the dining room, more confused and torn than she'd been during his seduction.

Maybe he really *was* only interested in the magic? Seducing her was merely a side amusement. *Or he stopped because he found out you're a virgin.* That made more sense. She had no skills or abilities in that department. Of course he'd lose interest in her.

She told herself that was fine as long as he still wanted to invest in the salon, which it sounded like he did. After all, he'd said they had a deal to conclude. If he could save the salon, she could harden her heart and forget what had happened. *Or hold onto it forever.* The one and only date she'd ever have. Best make the most of the memory. Signaling the waitress, she said, "I'd like to see the menu again, please."

Damned if she wasn't going to order the most expensive thing on it.

Ophir swirled his wine and studied Tanika over the rim of the glass, so many thoughts warring within him, he didn't know where to begin. She'd called her djinn a demon. A creature. And she wanted him dead, even at the expense of her own deepest wish. That was powerful magic in and of itself. An unfulfilled wish explained so much; the magic embedded within her cells, the reason he couldn't read her like he could other humans. The attraction pulled at him stronger than any portal ever had. Stronger than even another djinn had any right to pull. The attraction only a mate could wield.

A mate who wanted to kill djinn.

He grew dizzy with memories of Emelda, who'd carried djinn blood within her, although she was unaware of it. Believing she might be worthy as a mate, he'd courted, wooed, and eventually revealed his true nature to her. She'd been a devout Muslim, and confessed his secret to the Imam, who in return incited a riot against Ophir's master. The outcry was explosive, for the master was disliked throughout the kingdom. Deep under the influence of the poppy, the master slept while the rioters set his chambers on fire. His ring-portal melted and his bones charred to ashes. Ophir could only stand amidst the flames and watch, unable to act without his master's orders. He'd closed his eyes against the volcanic intensity released with the destruction of the portal. Shuddered as the fire raged throughout the palace. And walked away as the flames spread over the rest of the city like a tsunami.

No one in the palace survived.

He blinked away the memory as the waitress removed his half-empty bowl of lobster bisque and set a plate fanned with enormous prawns before him. Loving a mortal was folly. He might as well fall in love with one of these shellfish. But fate seemed intent on driving him forward. Tanika was irresistible.

She'd ordered a prime rib with fermented garlic cream. He found it amusing that she'd decided to order her own meal after their intimacy. As if she, too, wanted to resist the extraordinary connection between them. She licked her lips and eyed his plate as if regretting her entree decision.

"Would you like to try one?" he asked, stabbing a succulent prawn with his fork and holding it out to her.

"Oh, I don't want to take away your dinner."

"Please." He stretched the fork across the intimately-sized table toward her mouth.

She hesitated only a moment, her gaze never leaving his, then leaned in to accept. The fork held too much for a single bite, and when he continued holding it toward her, she grinned delightedly, finishing the morsel off. "Thank you. That was amazing."

"I didn't say it was free." He cocked a brow at her.

She looked at him wide-eyed and frozen, like a deer in the headlights.

Damn, her innocence was sexy. He pointed his fork at her plate. "I want a taste of your prime rib."

"Oh!" She laughed nervously and pushed her plate toward him. "Oh, sure. That makes sense."

He looked down at the plate then back at her. Smiling in a way he knew women couldn't resist, he opened his mouth expectantly. Wooing her might be folly, but he couldn't help himself. She was so lovely sitting there across from him, refreshing in so many ways. His honest gypsy. He didn't have supernatural hearing, but he swore he could hear her heartbeat racing like a mouse's. Making her uncomfortable was a delightful game.

"Oh!" She hurriedly cut a slice of prime rib and lifted it with her fork, hand trembling.

"You're adorable when you're nervous." He allowed her to shove the too-huge bite in between his lips. The beef was quite nice, tender and flavorful and seasoned with a hint of lemon.

"Is *this* normal for a business dinner?" She stared at her fork as if it were a foreign object.

Still chewing, he shook his head slowly, eyes never leaving hers. She'd known the answer before she'd asked it, of course. Mortals couldn't help playing the game.

A series of emotions contorted her face, as if she wasn't quite sure which to settle on. Brows pinched and lips pale, she cleared her throat. "Listen, I know we kind of got off on the wrong foot. But like I told you, what happened back there," she twitched her gaze toward the kitchens, "can never happen again. I can't be in a relationship. I want to talk about the salon. Business."

So they were back to this. Business instead of pleasure. She was a stubborn one, for sure. Her rock-solid refusal to fulfill her wish must be driving her djinn insane. He realized he was jealous of this unknown djinn having access to her any time, day or night. "Okay, then. I want you to be my personal psychic. On-call twenty-four seven."

Her brows drew even closer together. "But I couldn't even read you."

"Exactly." He bit into a prawn, chewing slowly. "So when you do see something, I know it'll be real. That's worth a lot to me."

Tanika narrowed her eyes. "I don't believe you."

This woman might be innocent when it came to men, but she'd obviously had a lot of experience with her djinn's trickery and double talk. He picked up an asparagus spear. No relying on a trust spell. No charming her with a come-hither. Perhaps right now the truth would serve him best. Yet the truth had cost him Emelda, and he didn't want to repeat that cascade of horror. A partial truth, then. He set down the asparagus and wiped his mouth with his napkin before proceeding. "What if I told you I can free you of your djinn?"

He'd been thinking about this ever since she'd revealed the unspent wish. Everything with djinn came at a price, and Ophir had wondered from time to time how he might convince a kinsman to allow him passage, since he had little to offer. Tanika's wish provided a unique opportunity. After decades trapped by an unfulfilled wish, her djinn was probably desperate to return home. Enough that he'd relinquish his claim on the portal if Ophir assumed the wish's debt. Tanika could not only be rid of her djinn, but Ophir could remain at her side. At least for the remainder of her short mortal life.

Tanika let her fork clatter to her plate. "I don't want him free. I want him dead."

The venom in her voice sent a chill through his immortal blood. The death of a djinn was a rare thing. More fierce in its repercussions than the destruction of a portal. Even the power-hungry djinn who hunted those weakened after procreation were cautious in their methods. What would she think if she ever found out Ophir was a djinn? He cleared his throat, vowing to himself not to let that happen. "I can send him away. Humans will never have to worry about him again."

She regarded him through narrowed eyes. "How do you know so much? How do you even know he's a djinn?"

His breath caught. He'd let that slip. She'd never called him a djinn, only a demon or a creature. "I've been drawn to magic my entire life," he said. "I've studied centuries of arcane knowledge. As soon as you said there was a wish involved, I knew."

Her shoulders relaxed a fraction. "He took advantage of a young child. Killed my family. Has basically held me hostage for almost two decades. I want him to suffer. "

"He won't be free. He'll be trapped in his own realm once again. Believe me, he'll suffer." The djinn was already suffering, his magic slowly draining away the longer he held the wish open, yet he was unable to close it. Djinn magic was a lawful thing, even though djinn nature could be chaotic. An agreement could be twisted, reinterpreted, even renegotiated, but never broken. Her djinn would return home a weakened thing, susceptible to other djinn.

She licked her lips, obviously still skeptical. "You could really banish him from Earth? Forever?"

"I can't promise forever, but he'll be weak. At the mercy of other djinn, and believe me, they are cruel. The likelihood of him acquiring another portal is slim."

"And what would happen to my wish?"

He scratched behind his ear, uncertain how to answer her. He had every intention of fulfilling her wish. And yet a part of him felt dirty that he'd use the wish to requite his own desire to mate her. She was mortal. Fragile. Finite. Ultimately, he'd be the one to suffer, left behind when she passed on. Djinn magic could not grant her immortality. A wish required a soul, and becoming immortal was contrary to the cost. "Wishes never go away. Whether or not yours comes true would be up to you."

Tanika stared past him a moment, her eyes glazed as if thinking about something. Her throat rippled as she swallowed. Then she rose so fast her chair clattered to the floor behind her. "I have to go. Now."

Spinning, she ran from the restaurant.

Ophir was on his feet, confused by her sudden turn of emotion. And then a familiar scent from behind him made him stiffen. "I wondered what had my little human in such a tizzy."

Ophir spun to face the voice. The scent of djinn magic assaulted him, but not the sweet anise coming from Tanika. This was a bitter acetone stink, the kind that came from a starving djinn. The bare-chested man standing in the middle of the restaurant gathered no odd looks, his magical glamour forcing the servers to skirt him without realizing why. He slid directly toward Ophir and took Tanika's seat at the small table. Age lines creased his face, a feature rarely seen on djinn, yet he still moved with the lithe confidence of one who had no fear of physical harm.

Slowly lowering himself back into his seat, Ophir faced his kinsman. Their kind seldom came face-to-face here on Earth, and when they did, it was often because warring masters caused them to clash. He hadn't been in the presence of another djinn in almost a millennia, and he found himself surprisingly misty-eyed with emotion.

His new table companion snatched up Tanika's wine glass with one gnarled hand, downing the contents in a single gulp. "Ah, I miss having a master who appreciates the finer things."

Picking up his own wine, Ophir sipped, keeping his face neutrally amused, despite the rapid pulse in his temples. "Greetings, kinsman. I'm called Ophir."

"Elim." The djinn waved a hand over his bare chest, conjuring an outdated dress jacket and cravat, then signaled the waitress for more wine. "You'll have to forgive me, Ophir." The djinn cut into Tanika's prime rib. "I have very limited time here, and am seldom near the pleasures of such fine cuisine."

Ophir wondered exactly how this djinn had come to be here, since he'd detected no portal on Tanika's person during their intimate encounter, and a djinn could not travel far from that point. But it wasn't a question he could ask outright. Talking to another djinn required finesse. A careful attention to detail so as not to be trapped when an inevitable deal was brokered; all interactions with djinn resulted in a deal. "Does she treat you so badly?"

The waitress appeared with a bottle and filled Elim's glass to the brim while he chewed in ecstatic delight. After swallowing, he met Ophir's gaze, brows lifting suggestively. "My voluptuous mortal offers all manner of decadent opportunities."

Possessiveness flared inside Ophir's chest, and he wanted to leap across the table to throttle the djinn for daring to hint at any sort of intimate knowledge of Tanika. Then he realized what Elim was doing—tempting him, possibly with an intention to trap him. Elim had to be looking to escape the deal with Tanika.

Smirking, Ophir pushed the bread basket across the table toward the hungry djinn. "She calls you her poltergeist."

Eyes hardening, Elim upended the bread onto his plate and sopped up the meat juice with a slice. "I see," he spoke around a mouth full of food. "Did she tell you her wish, then, too?"

Ophir nodded placidly.

"Interesting. No matter." He washed down his mouthful with wine. "The mortal's biological clock is ticking. I'm confident I can bring her around soon. Perhaps you can tell me why you might be skulking around another djinn's master?"

Ophir sighed and set his glass down, dabbing at his

mouth with a napkin. It was too soon to reveal he had no master. That he was seeking a portal. Revealing his desire made it a target, easy leverage, just as Elim's predicament was leverage right now. Yet it wasn't enough. Ophir needed to strengthen his own position and make Elim more insecure. "It's good you have your master under control. These humans have such fickle desires, don't they? So short-lived and unaware of what they truly want, especially the young. How old was Tanika when she made her wish?"

Gaze narrowing, the djinn paused, his teeth buried in a hunk of bread. He set the morsel down and slid a glance left, then right. "I don't feel the pull of a portal nearby. Where's your master?"

Blood thrumming in his ears, Ophir narrowed his eyes at the other djinn. "I could ask the same of you."

"You need to be on your way." Elim stuffed a full slice of bread into his mouth, making his withered cheeks bulge.

"Is this your mistress's territory, then? Is she sultana of the realm?" Ophir chuckled, imagining Tanika enrobed in a translucent silk kaftan and bejeweled head-to-toe. He might have to facilitate that fantasy once this was all over. "I do not envy you, beholden to such a master."

Rising, the djinn flared his nostrils. "Are you saying you have no master? What sort of power have you found?" The djinn's body rippled and began to fade. With an indignant huff, he scowled down at himself, snatched one final slice of bread from his plate, and was gone, taking with him the bitter acetone scent of his magic.

Janika didn't look back as she fled the restaurant and her gleefully grinning djinn. All she could think about was dragging the monster as far away from Ophir as possible, thankful he could only appear in her near proximity since she'd put him into the safe deposit box. If she moved fast enough, perhaps Elim couldn't even get a clear picture of who she'd been dining with. How many people had he twisted and warped in an attempt to make them suit her wish? This was why she didn't date. Why she stayed away from men. Why did her demon have to ruin everything?

During her early years, her demon had only appeared to annoy her, but upon her eighteenth birthday, and her rejection of her initial suitor, he'd begun causing real trouble. Her first apartment building had experienced electrical shorts and constant outages, with his constant reminder that all her troubles could end if she'd only accept the wish. The next place she lived had to be condemned when they found black mold. A duplex she rented had burned to the ground. Then there were the tricks he'd played on poor Mr. Daniels, putting weevils in the flour and replacing the sugar with salt.

Reaching the sidewalk, she realized darkness had fallen, and the street lights cast deep shadows across the cars parked along the curbs. She dug out her cell phone and dialed a taxi, giving it an address several doors away. A year ago, after the incident with Mr. Daniels, she'd marched to the bank and rented a safe deposit box, hoping to restrict her demon's access to her neighbors through distance. Renting the box had cost every spare penny she had, but she was nervous enough about letting the pendant out of her sight. She wanted to ensure it was as safe as she could make it. Elim had laughed at her plan, threatening to override the security systems and allow thieves into the security vault. With great pleasure, she'd reminded him that even if he did end up in another's hands, he had nothing to offer a new master; he could grant no wishes until hers had been fulfilled.

Ahead, she spotted a yellow taxi pulling to the curb

and ran to meet it. Clambering into the back seat, she gasped out her home address to the driver, still recalling the moment she'd sealed the safe deposit box over the pouch with the necklace. Elim had been standing beside her, cursing. Then his voice had ceased as if she'd flicked off a radio. He'd disappeared as if he'd never existed.

For months, she'd believed herself free of him.

Then he'd reappeared in her kitchen, snarling with fury and breaking every dish she owned. Apparently, the metal box interfered with his ability to use the pendant as a gateway. As dishes crashed all around her, and his hot breath fanned her face, he informed her he'd not be shut away so easily.

The taxi dropped her off outside her condo and she headed through the narrow courtyard. At least the demon's power had been diminished by the safe deposit box. He could only appear in her immediate vicinity, and couldn't tarry long enough to cause trouble. At least, not much trouble. It also took him time to recuperate between appearances, so she knew she had a little breathing room now. But running out like that had probably ruined Ophir's confidence in her as a business partner. She should've known this would happen. Sooner or later, the demon always discovered her plans and found a way to pollute them. She was a fool to hope any of her dreams might come true.

Opening her front door, she was surprised by the demon clucking his tongue. "Naughty, naughty girl. You certainly like to dance with the devil. What would your mother think?"

Her stomach roiled. Somehow he always knew how to make a bad situation worse. Usually by invoking her mother. Well two could play at that game. He was always complaining she kept nothing in the house worth eating, hurling her rice crackers and diet protein powders to the floor like a petulant child. The sumptuous restaurant must have driven him crazy jealous. "How long did you get to smell the food before you faded away, poltergeist?"

For once, he seemed unruffled by her jab. "Tell me, what did Ophir offer you?"

Shit. He'd managed to talk to Ophir long enough to learn his name. Had he managed to change him, too? To bend him to suit her wish? Now she could never trust another interaction with Ophir again. She stalked past Elim to the kitchen without answering, leaving the lights off in case he decided to start smashing light bulbs.

"Send him away." Elim trailed behind, feet making no sound on the scratched linoleum. "I'll beat whatever he's offering. Do you know how rare it is to be granted a second wish?"

"I don't want anything from you. Ever. You're a

monster and I'll see you in hell." She wanted to make tea, but didn't feel like having boiling water nearby if Elim got angry. Opening the fridge, she searched for a diet soda.

"Yet you'll deal with *him?*"

She didn't understand the venom in his voice, but she liked making him angry. "We're in negotiations."

"Over what?" His voice was harder than usual. Clipped. Dare she say nervous? Ophir had said he could banish the djinn. Could it be true? This was the first time she ever recalled Elim asking her to send someone away, especially an eligible bachelor.

In the yellow light streaming from the open fridge, she took in the exaggerated lines around his eyes and mouth. Did he look more craggy than usual? His hands were balled into fists at his sides. Whatever Ophir'd told Elim had frightened him enough to make him discount a potential husband. *Good.* She smirked and took a long drink of her soda. "He wants to invest in the salon."

"Invest?" The flesh around his eyes twitched. "What does that mean?"

"I imagine he'll be spending a lot of time around here. He wants to become a partner and help the salon start making money."

The demon began to chuckle. "He told you he wants to make money?"

She blinked nervously. Ophir hadn't said he wanted to make money. He'd asked her to be his personal psychic. *In spite of the fact that I couldn't read him.* Distrust flared again. "Why, what did he tell you he wanted?"

Elim laughed harder, his wide mouth revealing blocky white teeth. "You don't know, do you?" He leaned in closer, eyes filled with deep purple fire. "Ophir is a djinn. Just. Like. Me."

The floor seemed to sway beneath Tanika's feet, and she groped for a dining chair to steady herself. "Wh-what?"

But her demon didn't answer. His laughter faded along with his body, and she was left standing in a dark kitchen wondering if she should cry or laugh hysterically.

A djinn? Really? What the fuck? Was she some sort of evil magic magnet?

She fisted her hands into her curls and screamed under her breath. She didn't need the neighbors calling the cops again. They had often enough while her demon was throwing one of his tantrums. Everyone in the building assumed she was schizophrenic, having violent domestic squabbles with herself.

Flopping into the kitchen chair, she threw her head back and stared at the ceiling. Ophir had arrived at the salon looking for somebody. For Elim? Did djinn make house calls on other djinn? She had no idea. Then there was his insistence that she go out with him. She pressed her thighs together as she remembered his hands all over her body, the wave after wave of indescribable pleasure he'd elicited in her. Was that merely part of some elaborate djinn scheme? For what? To convince her to become his personal psychic?

She laughed out loud, leaning forward to lay her head on the kitchen table. *A psychic for a djinn. Hilarious.*

Then she bolted upright. Maybe that was double speak for him asking her to be his master? That's kind of what Mom had been for Elim, using her psychic abilities to sell his wishes to the highest bidder while abstaining from making any wishes herself. Had Ophir been proposing the same kind of deal? A ball of dread enveloped her stomach. No way in hell would she ever agree to that.

But he hadn't asked for anything like that. He'd offered to banish her djinn. Was that because a person could only be a master for one djinn at a time? Her mom would've known. But Mom was dead. She realized she was panting and took another swig of soda, trying to calm her heart. Perhaps not all djinn were like Elim. What if her demon—her djinn—was, like, a djinn felon, or something? Ophir might be a sexy djinn cop, out to capture his man and sweeping the girls off their feet along the way.

She shook her head. *You've been reading way too many romance novels, Tanika.* If Ophir was a djinn cop, he would've captured Elim at the restaurant. *Unless Elim faded too fast?* She had run away fairly quickly.

Dammit. It was time to stop arguing with herself and make a plan. For all she knew, Elim was lying about the entire thing, and Ophir wasn't a djinn at all. Her demon could be trying to use reverse psychology on her, to trick her into fulfilling her own wish. It wouldn't be the first time he'd attempted that tactic. She needed to talk to Ophir again. Give him the opportunity to explain his side of things.

Unfortunately, she'd just fled from a date with a guy she knew nothing about. Not a phone number, an address—hell, not even his last name. What kind of idiot was she? Taken in by a set of broad shoulders, sexy chocolate-colored eyes, and a lightning-fast Ferrari. He was probably long-gone from the restaurant by now.

Looking around to be sure she was alone, she opened the cupboard and pulled a box of rice crackers from the back shelf. Beneath the cardboard-flavored disks, she'd hidden a bag of miniature peanut butter cups from Elim's prying eyes. If Ophir was indeed a djinn, then good riddance. And if he was still interested in investing, he'd return to the salon tomorrow.

Sitting down at the table, she unwrapped the first one of the night and put the entire thing in her mouth. Chocolate solved everything right?

8

Unsure of exactly what he was after, Ophir tracked Tanika down. The task proved quite easy, even without magic. Her name was unusual enough that a quick Google search, cross-referenced against the city's DMV records, yielded her home address. Why rush to go back to more companions like Elim when he'd just found a woman like Tanika? Now he stood at her door with a bag of takeout in one hand and a fresh bottle of wine in the other. He pressed the doorbell and waited.

Footsteps vibrated behind the door, then a long pause, as if she was considering pretending to not be at home. No doubt Elim had already informed her of the situation, poisoning her against a fellow djinn. *She wants to kill her djinn.* The reminder should cool Ophir's blood, but Elim was kind of a dick—most djinn were. *Plus she's mortal.* None of it mattered. He couldn't talk himself out of seeing her again.

Holding the bag of take out in front of the peephole, he called out, "We never got to finish our meal."

Another beat of silence, then the bolt clicked and the door swung open, stopping short on the security chain. Through the crack, Tanika's eyes were round, and her ample breasts heaved a little too quickly. Elim must've indeed told her, and now she was afraid. Ophir decided honesty would be the best approach to win her over. "I'm sorry I didn't tell you."

She seemed to wilt, like a fresh-cut flower in the sun. "So you are a... a djinn?"

For the first time in his long existence, Ophir wished he could answer differently. He had to resist the urge to take her into his arms and apologize. "Yes."

"Why are you here?"

Again he held up the bag and grinned. "To finish our meal." Her lips thinned, and he realized he'd been too playful. He dropped his arm, allowing his expression to become serious. "I apologize. I'm here to talk. I swear to you I'll tell the truth. Whatever you want to know."

"Why. Are. You. Here?" she repeated.

He took a deep breath, shooting a glance up and down the courtyard before answering. "I came here looking for a portal." The portal might be what had brought him here, but it was no longer the reason he sought her out. If djinn weren't immune to their own magic, he might've wondered if a wish had brought them together.

The shielding in her eyes faded. Deep within her gaze, he thought he detected a hope that matched his own. "You don't have one of your own?"

"I'd really prefer not to have this conversation standing in the courtyard. Do you mind if I come in?"

She licked her lips, hesitating only a heartbeat. Then she loosened the chain and held the door wide for him, pointing down the short hallway. "The kitchen's through there."

"Thank you." He brushed by without touching her, forcing himself to be satisfied with only a deep breath of her citrus and anise aroma. Inside, he examined the small apartment. The place was oddly devoid of furniture and decoration other than an overstuffed couch loaded with fluffy pillows and a flat screen TV bolted to the wall. He sifted the air for magic, seeking signs of Elim's portal. The apartment smelled of anise, just like the salon, but it hadn't been coated in an oily glamour to dull its appeal.

The kitchen proved to be similarly plain, holding only a small folding table and two folding chairs. On the table sat an open bag of candy, empty metallic wrappers rolled into little balls and piled to one side. One cupboard hung open, revealing two cans of soup and a box of rice crackers.

Setting the takeout on the table, he asked, "Are you moving?"

"What?"

"This apartment looks... barren."

"Oh. Things just... tend to get broken a lot here at home."

He clenched his jaw, hating the thought of anything she valued being broken. No wonder she called her djinn a poltergeist. He opened the Styrofoam carton, allowing the rich aroma of butter chicken to fill the air. "I hope you like Indian food. There was a little hole-in-the-wall place along the way, and it smelled so good, I had to stop."

She remained standing. "Please, just tell me what you want from me."

Right to the point, then. The time for pleasantries was over. His heart broke a little that the intimacy they'd developed at the restaurant was over, but perhaps if he regained her trust, she'd let him back in. First things first, however. Once again he sifted the air for Elim. "Is he here?"

She narrowed her eyes. "He's locked away. Why?"

Her words sent a chill down his spine. Just as contact with metal disabled his casting, a portal completely surrounded in enough metal could be rendered inert. No wonder the other djinn had looked so gaunt. Ophir had assumed it was merely the drain of an unfulfilled wish held open for so many years. Now he realized it had to be because Elim had not only been unable to broker more wishes for energy, he'd not had enough food to replenish his corporeal body. He was literally burning his own magic reserves like a human burned fat. "How did he come to the restaurant?"

"He uses the wish connecting us like a conduit." Her skin looked a little green at the words. "But he says it takes a lot of energy. Twice in one night is a lot. I doubt he'll be back again soon."

Ophir'd never heard of such a possibility; Elim must be a very powerful djinn. Thinking about Elim using her like that made Ophir's blood run hot. "Is he hurting you?"

She cocked her head, arms crossed. "I believe you said you'd answer my questions. So far I'm the only one answering anything."

"Fair enough." He took the other seat and placed a second plastic fork on the empty side of the table in invitation. "I'm looking for a way home, and Elim's is the first portal I've come this close to finding. Probably because your wish is keeping the portal ajar."

"What happened to your portal?" Her brows furrowed.

"Destroyed." He put a bite of chicken into his mouth, but she was looking at him with such concentration, he hardly tasted it.

"So you're free?"

He swallowed. "Free? I suppose so. I'm not tied to a portal. But I can't get home, either."

She perched hesitantly on the opposite chair and shifted her gaze to the empty countertops. "Do you grant wishes?"

He watched her obviously forced nonchalance. Was she searching for a way to break Elim's bond? "I can't negate one wish by granting another if that's what you're asking."

"That's not what I asked. I want to know if you..." Her breath shook as she finished her sentence, "harvest souls."

Wariness settled hard against his breastbone. She wasn't hoping for another wish, then. She was searching for a reason to hate him. His djinn nature urged him to spin a vague answer that could be interpreted multiple ways. She'd asked in present tense, so he could honestly answer no. But that wouldn't be the real truth she was looking for. And he'd promised to tell her the truth. He felt as bound to that promise as if he'd made a deal for a wish. *You've been among mortals too long,* he thought to himself, even as he said, "Not anymore."

After a short pause, she asked, "But you used to."

"I will not lie. I did." He watched her lovely face for signs of hatred. Instead, he saw guarded curiosity.

She fiddled with her hands in her lap. "Why did you stop?"

He cleared his throat. This was another question that had both an easy answer, and a difficult one. He decided on a halfway point. "After eight hundred years, I no longer feel the addictive pull."

She seemed to consider. "What you really mean is you can't."

He had to appreciate her intelligence. She'd obviously had much experience with her djinn's double-talk. "I can perform small magic to suit my own purposes. However, the heavy magic required to grant a wish is beyond me."

"Because you lost your portal?"

"A portal provides a connection to the deeper magic, yes."

Once again she crossed her arms, gaze so intense it threatened to ignite anything flammable it touched.

"That's why you need me. You want to use my djinn's portal and resume trading wishes for souls."

"No," he denied, although his mind spun with contradictions. He'd been searching for a portal so long, he'd forgotten his motivation. Was it to resume his previous life? Or was it to escape the eternal grief of losing those around him to mortality? He hadn't really thought about what would happen after he located a portal. All he knew at this moment was that he wanted Tanika to be happy. "I want to help you escape the trap you find yourself in."

She laughed, her face lined with derision. "You're basically a djinn forced into in rehab. Why should I trust you? Or for that matter, why should you trust yourself? Drug addicts think they're free, as well, until they have the opportunity to use again."

Ophir stiffened, once again shocked by this mortal who could see things more clearly than anyone—djinn or human—he'd ever met. Was he simply an addict? The long ago memory of souls he'd taken, the dramatic rush of energy and power, washed over him in a way he'd not experienced in a very long time. A remembered hunger almost impossible to fight. The absolute euphoria of consuming a mortal soul.

And he realized it paled in comparison to the way he felt around Tanika.

Tanika's nails bit into her palms as she waited for Ophir's reaction to being called an addict. With all her heart, she wanted to believe not all djinn were like Elim. But Ophir had admitted to harvesting souls, and the way Elim talked about the experience made her believe it must feel like a giga-hit of meth. How could any djinn who'd experienced that reject an opportunity if it came along again?

Ophir's features clouded, and he seemed lost in thought. Then he bent over the butter chicken and inhaled, eyes closed as if in meditation. "The combination of spice in this dish is like nothing found on my world." Opening his eyes, he wrapped his long fingers delicately, almost reverently around the carton. "When I am surrounded by sensations like this, I feel... almost human."

She remained frozen with her arms crossed, almost afraid to move. The sensual way he enjoyed the aroma made it difficult to concentrate on his words. The conversation was serious, yet all she could think about was the way his big hands caressed the carton.

"My time here among mortals, who can't take a single day for granted, who manage to create wonders in spite of their limited individual existence, has changed me." He released the carton and leaned back in his chair. "Djinn are only creative in deal making. We don't produce things, don't innovate solutions. From the phone I used to Google your address, to the convertible I drove here, there are no limits to human imagination. You excel over and above my race. Taking even one of you before your time is finished is a waste of potential."

God help her, she wanted to believe him. But he still hadn't actually answered the question, and she knew from her dealings with Elim how tricky words could be. "That's just like saying how pretty a cake is right before you cut it."

That elicited a laugh, not the gloating kind she was used to from her djinn, but one of pleasure, eyes squeezed shut while he shook his head. "You are truly delightful, Tanika. Both charming and quick-witted. And you are correct. Let me say in plain words what I mean." He met her gaze, his dark eyes filled with intense purple light. "After eight hundred years among humans, I find the thought of taking a human soul repulsive. I personally don't ever want to do that again."

She took a deep breath, considering what he'd just said, looking for loopholes. Elim would bend words, but he prided himself that he never lied. Apparently truthfulness was a djinn value or something. She couldn't find any wiggle room in what Ophir said. Hesitantly, she offered, "Promise me you won't harvest anyone again, and I'll believe you."

His gaze remained steady. "I will not harvest a mortal soul ever again."

Shoulders relaxing, she realized she could finally take a full breath. "All right. Then why are you looking for a portal?"

The purple light infusing his gaze flickered. "I... don't know that I am."

She frowned, uncertain all over again. "Isn't that what you claimed when I let you though the door?"

"It is. But you've made me rethink that goal."

Her belly tightened with anticipation. What goal might a djinn have, other than harvesting souls? Unless... "Wait, I know what's going on." She thrust up a hand. "Elim's cast a spell on you to make you complete my wish."

"Impossible." Ophir shook his head. "Djinn are immune to each other's magic, at least here on Earth."

A wave of relief flooded her. She wanted Ophir's attention to be real, not the product of some charm. "Are you sure?"

He smiled. "I'm sure. I'm here to save you from your djinn."

Maybe he is *with the djinn police.* "How?"

"Elim's wasting away under the wish's burden, and would probably do almost anything to be free of his debt."

She sneered. "He would. He's offered to renegotiate our deal many times." Her temper flared at the thought of all the things he'd suggested. "But like I told you in the restaurant, I don't want him free. I want him dead."

Ophir cocked his head. "That won't bring back your mother."

His words hit her like a blow to the stomach. "I know that. But I can at least be damned sure that monster never harms another human being." She fought back self pity. She'd resolved to follow this path years ago, and wasn't about to let another tricky djinn talk her out of it.

"You're not only refusing your wish, you know. Elim'll torture you until the day you die." Ophir leaned forward with his elbows on the table. "Did you know he's put a glamour on the salon? He's dulled it to make it less appealing to customers."

"Bastard." She slumped back in her chair and scowled, hands going limp on the table. "I knew he'd done something, but he'd never admit it."

"What if I send him back to my dimension? Permanently? So he can never return to this realm?" He reached across the table and enveloped one of her hands with his. "Would that satisfy your quest to protect humanity?"

His touch set her blood on fire. *Focus, Tanika.* "You said you can't access strong magic without a portal. Plus he's immune. How do you plan to beat him?"

"The way all djinn deal with one another. A deal."

"What kind of deal?"

He licked his lips. "I believe I may be able to assume his debt."

Her heart stopped beating for a moment. "As in... you become my djinn?"

"I'd take up ownership of the portal, yes."

"I knew it!" She jerked her hand away, betrayal burning through her.

"I meant it when I promised to never harvest another mortal." His gaze remained locked with hers, but he withdrew his hand. "But I can't think of another way to break Elim's hold on you."

She was still coming to grips with meeting a second djinn, let alone trust his motives. And yet some part of her wanted to trust everything about Ophir. The way his touch could make her brain turn to pudding was uncanny. Suspicion blossomed in her chest. "Are *you* casting a spell on me?"

"I am not. In fact, I can't." His response was long, drawn out, and sexy. "I've never met a human like you."

Her breath fluttered in her throat. "What do you mean?"

He leaned forward, the cheap folding chair creaking as he shifted. "It could be the magic of your wish infusing you, or perhaps you carry a trace of djinn blood."

"As in, a djinn was my ancestor?" Her stomach flip-flopped, the chocolate she'd eaten earlier churning uncomfortably in her stomach. The idea of having ancestral ties to a djinn made her physically nauseous.

He shrugged. "It's possible. During the early years of our ventures to Earth, before it was discovered that mortal souls could be consumed, a few djinn found human mates and bonded. After so many millennia, however, the remaining bloodlines are very thin."

Even more than the prospect of being part djinn, talking to Ophir about mates and children made her uncomfortable. She swallowed, squaring her shoulders. "So I'm a special snowflake or whatever. That still doesn't explain why you care so much about my happiness."

He rose, his body slow and languid, and moved around the table to stare down at her. "Consider it selfish. I don't want you running away from me every time I look at you because you're afraid of a wish."

If she'd been standing, her knees would've buckled

under his hungry gaze. His cologne had been masked by the butter chicken earlier, but now he was standing close enough to bump her knees, and his masculine scent filled her with heady desire. With one hand, he pushed the folding table aside, the rubber-capped feet squeaking against the linoleum, and moved into the space it had occupied. Squatting, he placed one hand on each of her knees.

Captured by his intense stare, she couldn't form words. A long, heart-stopping moment passed. Slowly, he pressed his body between her unresisting thighs, pushing them open until his breath fanned her face. He teased his tongue along the seam of her mouth, sending a shiver straight to her navel. Quivering, she felt her lips part to accept him.

Heaven help her, this man turned her very thoughts to jelly, not to mention her body.

He nibbled her top lip first, then her bottom, as if sampling her for the first time. Her hands crept to his shoulders, slid up and caressed the back of his neck. A tilt of his head, and his mouth captured hers, tongue running along her teeth before stroking long and firm inside her. She clung to him, letting him lead her in an erotic dance, his hands sliding up her thighs to rest at the bend of her hips.

A hungry noise escaped him, telling her how badly

he wanted her, sending rockets of anticipation deep into her core. She hooked her ankles around his waist, thrilling at the rigid length of his erection pressing against her sex. He tilted forward, grinding himself against her clit and deepening the kiss. Remembering the way he'd coaxed an orgasm from her at the restaurant made her core quiver with excitement. What they were doing was dangerous. Forbidden. It only made her want Ophir more, to experience all he had to offer. To accept his promise of freedom.

"Tanika," he groaned against her lips. Sliding both hands under her bottom, he rose, keeping her entwined about him like a starfish. His muscles rippled as he moved, sure and secure even with her added weight. As if he'd been to her apartment a million times, he easily carried her through the living room to her bedroom, nudging open the door with one foot and lowering her to the bed. All the while never breaking contact with her hungry lips.

The sound of someone clearing his throat froze them both.

"Looks like I got here just in time." Elim's voice grated through the room like breaking glass.

9

Ophir straightened to face the other djinn, his nerves on fire with magic. The food must've bolstered Elim's reserves. Tanika scurried to the bedside lamp and clicked it on, revealing her djinn with his arms crossed, deep scowl lines cut into his face.

"How are you here again so soon?" she said breathlessly.

"I was worried for you." Elim's voice dripped sarcasm. "I am, after all, indebted to your happiness."

"If that were true, you'd keel over and die," she spat out.

Rolling his eyes, Elim turned his attention to Ophir. "This is not the situation I expected to find you in. What are you playing at, Ophir?"

Ophir chuckled, stretching his neck side to side and

smoothing his shirt across his chest, thinking carefully about his words. "You hinted at Tanika's... pleasurable... opportunities when we spoke at the restaurant. I was curious." He sat on the bed, bouncing slightly as if testing the springs. "Since I'm immune to your magic, I thought I'd offer her pleasure with no strings attached. Now if you'll excuse us, we'd prefer not to have an audience."

To his surprise, Tanika didn't balk at his crudeness. She pointed to the door. "Yes, Elim. Leave."

Elim's body seemed to vibrate, rippling as he leveled his glowing, purple gaze at his master. "You're not the kind of woman who can have a one night stand and walk away without regrets."

Tanika sniffed. "How would you know?"

"I saw to that with the way you were raised. Loving, moral adoptive parents. A family to teach you how to achieve your wish." His eyes glowed with purple embers. "I took care of you."

Ophir laughed. "Took care of her? More like you were nervous. That must've cost a lot of energy, reinforcing the wish's hold on her."

Elim's eyes narrowed, turning their purple glow to slits. "A poor deal, I admit. We've all made them. And she refuses to renegotiate." He licked his lips and cocked his head slightly. "You could help me. Convince her to complete the wish."

Ophir yawned as if growing bored with the conversation. Yet inside he was thrilled. Elim was making this deal so easy. "That would be a costly bargain, my friend. She's quite adamant she wants you dead."

"Everyone has a price." Spittle flew from Elim's lips. "Just find out what hers is."

"Mm. Your predicament *is* intriguing." Ophir rolled his head to look at Tanika where she still cowered by the lamp, her olive skin ashen. "What would it take, Tanika?"

She visibly gulped, her gaze meeting his. A heartbeat passed. Then ten. Finally, she shifted her attention back to Elim. "I want you to leave Earth and never interact with another human again."

Elim's nostrils flared. "That's no kind of deal. You get what you want and I get nothing."

"Nothing?" She stomped forward as if she was going to attack, but stopped at the corner of the mattress. "You took my mother and grandmother! You already had your payment!"

Ophir rose, joining her. She was magnificent when she was angry. He wouldn't be surprised to see a flicker of lavender light in her eyes. He smirked at his fellow djinn. "She's right, Elim. I'd take her deal."

Eyes blazing, Elim curled his lips and took a deep breath. Weak as the djinn might be, he still seemed to swell with power. "What's in this for you, Ophir? Why are you here? Not merely for a piece of mortal ass."

A rumble of warning rose from Ophir's throat. Before he could speak, Tanika elbowed past, glowering at her djinn. "You're just angry I've found myself a friend with benefits, and there's nothing you can do about it."

The bedside lamp popped and went out, leaving the room lit only by the flames in Elim's eyes. "Do not mock me, mortal. I've been patient until now."

Tanika seemed to be on a roll, though. "What're you going to do, poltergeist? Dull my scissors? Swap the colors on my hair dye? You have no real power left. You're just a shell of whatever monster you used to be."

Elim roared, throwing his hands out as if to strangle her. Tanika reeled, throwing her hands up before her while the djinn roared, "I'll burn down the salon with Birdie inside if that's what it takes!"

Ophir lunged, knocking the djinn aside. Elim wouldn't actually harm Tanika, not with the wish hanging between them, but Ophir refused to allow her to be intimidated. He stood nose-to-nose with Elim, his breath ragged. "Not as long as I'm around."

Elim's eyes grew wide. Then his mouth spread into a leer. "She's not just a piece of ass for you, is she?" He stepped back and put both hands on his scrawny hips, a chortling laugh rolling out of him. "I thought mating humans was a thing of the past for our kind, yet here you are, proving me wrong. You do realize she's mortal, right? You're tying yourself to a mate who will wither and die."

The room suddenly felt devoid of air. Elim was right. Tanika was destined for death, just like every other human being Ophir had ever met. Just like Emelda. And no wish could ever change that. What kind of fool djinn was he to fall in love with a mortal not once, but twice? Hadn't he learned his lesson the first time?

He glanced at Tanika across the shadowed room. New terror gripped his soul as he realized the truth of it. He no longer cared about the portal. No longer needed to escape Earth. All he wanted was Tanika, to have and to hold for the rest of her life. Then he would gladly take Elim's place beside her in the grave. No matter what else happened between now and eternity, Tanika was his. He didn't want to think about the what-ifs. He only wanted her. She was his, for her lifespan and beyond.

Still laughing, Elim flicked his hand in dismissal.

"But who am I to judge if you want to do my job for me? Have at it, lovebirds. I'll be waiting."

With that, the djinn popped out of sight.

Tanika remained utterly silent, staring into the dark at the spot her demon had just vacated. She felt light-headed. First she'd been reeling from finding out Elim'd orchestrated her adoptive parents, which completely upended her interpretation of her childhood. Then she'd slammed up against another loss when the demon physically threatened Birdie, which meant that to protect her friend, she'd have to sever yet another relationship. And finally, this business about Ophir wanting her for a mate.

That one was hardest of all to believe. Mate sounded a heck of a lot more permanent than husband.

Hesitantly, she moved to the wall switch and flicked on the overhead light. The stricken expression on Ophir's face told her he was in as much shock as she was. Her heartbeat felt weak and thready as she whispered, "What's he talking about?"

Ophir sat on the edge of the bed and then fell backward as if he could no longer hold himself upright.

Staring at the ceiling, he said, "For eight hundred years, I've seen mortals come and go. Learned to distance myself from caring. All I've dreamed of is going home, of leaving this realm of mortality and death for good." He turned his head against the comforter to spear her with his gaze. "Yet now I find I cannot bear missing one microsecond of your very short life."

His words exposed her heart to an unfamiliar rawness—hope. She held a brief mental image of a house and a yard, Ophir playing ball with the kids, family picnics. A life of joy. He might as well have just uttered wedding vows.

She shook her head violently, trying to rid herself of the daydream. What was she thinking? Djinn probably didn't even have weddings. "Please don't. I can't. You know I can't."

He sat up again, face hard as steel. "You can if we destroy the portal."

Her mouth dropped open. For some reason she'd believed destroying a portal was impossible. But Ophir was proof it could be done. "Won't that just free him like you are?"

"Not if you destroy it while he's on the other side."

"Couldn't he find another portal and come back for revenge?"

"Portals are extremely rare. I doubt Elim will ever find a way to visit Earth again."

She bit her lip, considering. Was it enough to banish the demon? How much longer could she hold out against her wish, especially with Ophir seducing her by his mere presence? Ophir's plan meant Elim couldn't bother humanity for a long, long time. Possibly forever. It also meant destroying his only way home. She shook her head. "I can't ask you to do that."

"You're not asking me. I'm asking you. Marry me, Tanika."

Her knees began trembling, the room spinning around her. She stumbled forward and sat, hard, on the mattress beside him. Pulling her toward him, he cleared a tangle of curls from her cheek with gentle fingertips. "I know this is sudden. It's sudden for me too, but a djinn knows when he's met his mate. If you'll have me, I'll be yours for the rest of time."

Tears filled her eyes, and she blinked furiously to clear her vision. She didn't want to lose sight of this gorgeous, amazing man who was more than she'd ever hoped for in a husband. Except for one thing—he wasn't human. He'd just reminded her he was over eight hundred years old. She knew djinn were immortal, but she'd never thought about the fact she and Ophir could never grow old together. The consequences of that fact took away her breath. "You mean for the rest of my life. When I'm gone, you'll be trapped here on Earth, alone."

He shook his head. "Djinn only mate once, and mates are bound much the same way you and Elim are now."

Either her ribcage had shrunk, or her heart swelled, because there didn't seem to be enough room inside her chest. "You mean you'll die?"

He shrugged and looked away. "Yes."

"No!" She sat up, cupping his angular cheek. He immediately cradled her knuckles, turning his face to kiss her palm. His breath was warm on her skin. Alive. More than alive. He was immortal. Something humans dreamed of. Schemed for. Nausea rose up inside her as she scrambled for her options. "You grant wishes. Can't you make me immortal?"

Lips still pressed to her palm, he smiled, but his eyes were pinched with sadness. He pulled her back down against him so her cheek rested against his chest. "Granting true immortality is beyond my power. The closest thing I could do is extend your life over and over." His voice grew brittle. "Assuming you could find a willing a mortal soul to pay the price."

She stiffened, remembering her mother's sacrifice.

Nausea roiled within her. "Have you granted such a wish before?"

"No." He squeezed her in reassurance. "I knew the possibility existed, but I never mentioned it as a solution when a master requested immortality."

Twisting, she looked into his face. "But you just told me."

His melted-chocolate eyes met hers. "I'm not concerned about you pursuing such a deal."

She swallowed, the urge to kiss him making her mouth tingle. His heartbeat was strong beneath her cheek. He knew her well, in spite of the fact they'd just met. She could envision spending the rest of her life with him. But she couldn't ask him to give up immortality. He'd regret it in the end. He needed to think about what he was losing. "Tell me about your home world."

Brow furrowing as if he was struggling to remember, he said, "It's impossible to describe in human language. A place of shifting ether and ebony ribbons of plasma. Djinn are beings of energy. We follow the plasma like gypsies on houseboats. We shift and deal, trading in energy. Our dimension is a realm of souls, if you will. A portal allows us to experience corporeal existence."

"To have a body, you mean?"

"Yes."

"Why would you want that?"

"Energy is like a drug to my people. Moving from matter to energy and back again is the most potent experience we have. Absorbing a human soul is indescribable bliss." His face flushed and he looked away as if ashamed to meet her gaze. "Once we discovered Earth, had a taste, it was impossible to go back. I think... I think I've been lucky to be here long enough to break the addiction. To become human."

She realized he meant it. He didn't want to go back to the way he was. She whispered, "Once the portal is gone, you'll be trapped here."

He pressed his lips to her forehead. "I can't recall a day I didn't long for a portal, and now you couldn't force me through if you tried." Pulling back, he lifted her chin, looking into her eyes. "A mortal life with you, Tanika, would be worth every moment."

His intensity made her nerves jangle. She'd lived so long in denial, she was uncomfortable with the idea of her wish being fulfilled. "What if I say no?"

He scrunched up his face, and then gently nipped her nose, turning her anxiety into laughter. "You're not getting rid of me that easy. I have to stick around and keep you out of trouble, whether you'll have me or not."

She wrapped her arms around his waist and squeezed, the hard planes of his body pressed against hers. The tips of her breasts ached where they crushed against him.

He slid his hands down along her spine and cupped her bottom, adjusting her to bring her even closer. The familiar touch on her body made her insides thrill. She was going to do this. She was going to accept her wish.

Moving her hand to the hem of his shirt, she slid her hand beneath to the rippled muscles of his back, shocked by her own brazenness. His skin tremored in response, and she felt the surge of his cock against her belly. Her core tightened in response. Anticipation. Primitive emotions roiled within her, and the spot between her legs grew unaccustomedly warm.

Lowering his face to hers, he claimed her mouth, his lips demanding. One hand gripping the back of her neck, he thrust his tongue deeply inside her, rolling it and tangling against her insecure responses. She worried she might do it wrong. What if she wasn't able to please him? She'd never even had a childhood boyfriend to practice with.

Ophir didn't seem to mind. His roving hand cupped one of her breasts, massaging her aching flesh while he kissed his way across her jaw and down the column of her throat. The contact sent jolts of desire down her spine and stirred butterflies in her stomach. His hand left her breast and smoothed its way down to her hip. In one swift move, he'd lifted her blouse, raising her from the mattress to sweep the garment over her head. Cool air tingled across her skin.

Now his hands had full access to her torso, the warmth of his touch branding her. His fingers teased little gasps of pleasure every time he cupped a breast or dipped beneath the waistband of her leggings. His teasing fingers circled around her back and unhooked her bra. The sudden release of the elastic band felt like it might set all her butterflies free. She loved it. Wriggling out of the straps, she prickled beneath his hungry gaze.

"Beautiful," he murmured, and rolled her to her back. He swooped down, swiping across one nipple with his wide tongue.

Sparks ignited, her areola tightening her nipple to an impossible peak while the other breast cried out for equal attention. He suckled, flicking the sensitive tip, and a pulse of pure pleasure skittered downward toward her core. He moved to the other breast and gave it the same treatment, until she was arching her back for more.

Then he pulled away, and she felt nothing but the weight of his stare for a few heartbeats. She opened her eyes and met his. The lust there was undeniable. Yet he didn't move. Only knelt above her, his legs straddling hers. Anticipation built. Was she supposed to do something? She shifted her gaze downward to his crotch, and her insides thrummed at the bulge in his jeans.

His sultry voice reached out to her. "Do you want something, Tanika?"

"Yes." She couldn't hold back her desire.

"What? Tell me."

She flicked her gaze up again, meeting his eyes. He wanted her to ask? To beg? To take?

"You never said yes. I want to know you're sure." His voice wrapped around her like a caress.

Oh. She licked her lips. "You. I want you."

He smiled a sexy, naughty grin. Slowly, his long fingers unbuttoned his shirt, exposing his hard pecs and molded abs. His skin was smooth, except for a fine line of hair below his belly button, pointing the way into the waistband of his jeans. He tossed the shirt aside, a waft of masculine cologne filling the air, and then he was hovering above her, his naked chest brushing her peaked nipples. She made an unintelligible noise, barely able to breathe.

Supporting himself on his elbows, he cupped her face and kissed her, tongue delving deeply as her hands explored his exposed skin. Her legs were still trapped between his knees, and she flexed her hips upward, like a flower straining to open. He clamped his legs tighter, as if telling her to wait, and continued to kiss her, exploring every millimeter of her mouth.

Slowly, he began rocking, ever so slightly, rubbing their naked chests together. Each teasing abrasion across her nipples made her squirm. A need was growing inside her. A deep, undefinable desire for his attention all over her body. But the kiss was so mesmerizing, she didn't want it to end.

As if sensing her frustration, he lifted one knee and pushed it between her legs. She grunted in surprise and then delight as he ground his thigh against her clit. It pulsed and throbbed, and she clamped her thighs over his leg and rocked her hips. He increased his rhythm to match her desire, bumping against her. One hand left her face and cupped her hip, holding her steady, strengthening the contact with her clit. Her need grew. Rose up over her like a physical thing. Quivered on the edge, and crashed down over her.

Moaning, she rode her orgasm, legs quivering. Before the wave fully subsided, he moved to her breasts, running his tongue in circles around first one areola, then the other. The bundles of nerves there sent electric shocks of pleasure to her already pulsing core, drawing out the cascading orgasm like a sigh.

His mouth trailed from her breasts down her belly, leaving damp kisses to prickle in the cool air. He dipped his tongue into her belly button before moving lower. Her leggings slid from her body, taking her panties along with them, and she lay completely naked before him. He knelt and blew warm air across her clit. She shivered.

"Ophir," she moaned, not sure what she meant by it. He took it as a question.

"Yes, my love?" He kissed her inner thigh, sending more electric tingles rocketing to her core.

She parted for him, his hands gently easing her thighs apart and up, claiming complete access to her. The brush of his touch on her curls left her quivering. Then his tongue split her lower lips, swiping upward from the well of her desire over her clit, circling before dipping downward once again. She held still, panting, waiting. He circled her clit once again, then clamped his lips over the nub and sucked. She arched, a moan of pleasure escaping her. God, he knew how to work her body. She pushed her sex more firmly against him, begging for more.

He groaned, and pressed his face into her, penetrating her with his tongue. Lost to him, she grabbed fistfuls of his hair and bent her legs higher to accept him. His palms massaged her thighs, thumbs circling the sensitive space where her ass met her legs and into the crease along both sides of her pussy. He sucked and nipped until she couldn't focus on anything except the need to come again.

One of his hands left her thighs and he pressed a finger into her, sliding in and out until her core tightened around him. She whimpered and squirmed, unsure if she needed to get away or beg for more. He thrust harder, deeper, adding a second finger, sucking hard.

Another orgasm whipped through her, waves traveling from deep inside to take control of her entire body, wracking her with convulsions of pleasure.

Still it wasn't enough. It was incomplete. Panting, she reached for him, wanting, wanting everything. "Please. Fuck me."

His lust-filled gaze captured hers as he knelt above her. With one wave of his hand, his jeans winked out of existence, and he was before her in full naked glory, cock pulsing high and thick. A moment of fear engulfed her. He looked so big. So hard. But then he was lying atop her, the line of his erection teasing her wet cleft while he once again soothed her with his kisses.

She tightened her grip on his shoulders, wriggling. His cock was so heated, so hard. And she wanted it. She wanted all of it. The smooth round head poised at her entrance, pressing but not penetrating. She arched into him, her body tight with anticipation and need. So close. And yet he remained frozen. Panting.

"You sure?" he asked.

"Yes," she gasped. "Please."

He kissed her at the same time he thrust forward. She gasped, the sharp burn both surprise and relief. He felt impossibly large, and yet impossibly right. He filled an emptiness inside her, completed her in a way she'd never imagined possible. Her heart raced and she gasped for breath.

"You feel so good." He pulled back and rolled his hips to work more of himself inside her. "Am I hurting you?"

She shook her head and sighed, accepting him, wanting him, fitting him. She reveled in the burn as more of him slipped inside her. He paused, only partially joined, and stroked his tongue slowly along her lips. Rocking, he stretched her, eased into her, each thrust pushing him deeper. The assault on her senses was impossible to resist. She spread her legs as far as she could, welcoming him. With one more steady push, his hips settled against her with satisfying finality.

"Perfect," he hung his head and panted. "Everything about you. So perfect."

She wrapped her arms around his shoulders and held him close, relishing the indescribable sensation of their joining. The awe of holding him inside her only lasted a moment. Then he pulled back and thrust again.

The burn was less, now dominated instead by lust. His slow strokes ignited her in a different way than his mouth or his fingers. A fuller, more complete sensation.

In and out he thrust, as she flexed to meet him until his skin was slapping against hers. She groaned every time he embedded himself inside her, and his panting drove her to a frenzy. Her core tightened around his cock, all burning and pain long forgotten. Dizziness consumed her, and every nerve seemed stimulated. He pushed her higher than she thought possible for the human body to experience. She couldn't breathe. Couldn't move. Her body seemed locked on the edge of her orgasm.

He groaned her name and somehow filled her deeper. She teetered, waves rolling through her, up and down her body, setting her trembling. With a grunt, Ophir thrust once more. Hot bursts of his release filled her, each pulse of his cock sending another rippling contraction through her body. The rolling waves seemed to go on for an eternity, their joint release ending only after he'd given her everything.

The world came into focus again around her. Ophir's hot, slick skin pressed to hers. His panting breath in her ear. The reassuring weight of him on top of her. Her breathing slowed. Peace filled her.

Contentment. What they'd just shared was nothing short of amazing.

"My beautiful, perfect Tanika."

She let out a tremendous gasp. "That was... that was..."

"Bonding. That's what that was. I'm sealed to you. Now rest and let me hold you."

She did rest, safe and at peace for the first time since making her horrific wish.

Ophir rolled off Tanika's body, and the loss of her warmth was sharp. Immediate. He tugged her against his chest, reclaiming the comfort he'd found in her arms. She murmured and snuggled her luscious backside against him. He wanted to stay here forever. But they had one last thing to do.

He whispered in her ear. "Wake up, my love. We have a portal to destroy."

She curled herself tighter into a ball. "Now?"

He reached down and pinched her ass, hard enough to elicit a yelp of surprise, but not enough to truly punish. "Yes, now. Your wish is complete. He'll take the first chance he can to hand the portal to a new master."

She bolted upright, the curve of her breasts

illuminated in the faint glow of dawn outside her bedroom window. "But the bank is closed."

"No better time to break in, then, is there?"

With a gleam in his eye, he rose and conjured his clothes back into place. She scrambled for her own, and he smirked, watching her slide her feet into her leggings.

"You could help, you know," she grumped.

"And miss out on your divine curves? I think not."

She flushed as rosy as the sunrise outside.

Once they were both clothed, he led them to the convertible, settling her into her seat before asking for directions.

"We have to go to Redmond."

He squeezed her knee and drove them to a nearby doughnut shop.

"Why are we stopping?" she asked.

"I'm going to use a lot of energy to create a crucible hot enough to melt the portal. Carbs loading'll help." While the tired young man behind the counter filled two coffees, Ophir picked out a dozen doughnuts. "What's your favorite?" he asked Tanika.

"Oh, none for me, thanks."

Tipping the young man a hundred, he handed the pastry box to Tanika so he could douse his coffee with sugar. She took a deep breath of the box top and moaned. "Just holding this is going to make me gain twenty pounds, you know."

At the passenger side door he held out the keys and relieved her of the box. "Will you drive so I can eat?"

Her eyes lit up. "Drive? Me? This is nothing like my Ford Escort."

"You'll do fine." He bit into a Bavarian cream, tangy sweet cream flooding his tongue, and pastry melting in his mouth. He held it close to her mouth. "Try this. Just a taste."

Licking her lips, she hesitated, then leaned in and took a demure bite. "Oh, God." She closed her eyes and let her head fall back against the head rest. "That's delicious."

He shoved the rest into his mouth and reached for another, feeling the slowly building energy settle into his bones.

"Are you really going to eat all of them?"

He waggled his eyebrows and nodded, amused by her censuring tone.

"Lucky." She put the car into drive, eased out of the parking spot, put on her blinker and looked both ways before pulling onto the nearly empty street.

He laughed around a mouthful of jelly doughnut. "You don't have to be so cautious."

"About the car? Or the doughnuts?"

"Either." He held the doughnut toward her, and this time she took a big bite. Raspberry filling dotted the corner of her perfect mouth. He leaned over to lick it off, thrilled at the way she turned into him to transform the move into a kiss. After a long moment, she pulled back and took a breath, waggling a finger at him.

"Don't distract the driver." A smile adorned her face as she stepped on the gas, lurching them forward.

They reached Redmond in record time, where the bank's two-story brick building cast a long shadow across the pavement. Tanika pulled into the parking lot, stopping in a far corner under a huge oak tree. Cutting the engine, she looked around. "Someone is going to notice this car."

Ophir gave her the last bite of a maple bar, then kissed the stickiness from her lips, savoring her flavor as much as the doughnut. "Don't worry about it." He opened the door and got out. "You can even leave the keys. Only the people I want to see my car see it. Come on."

Taking her hand, he strode to the front door, flicked his fingers, and the locks released. He'd disabled the security cameras and alarms the moment he'd seen the First National sign. Luckily all these were small spells. He was going to need every reserve once they reached the portal.

"What about the guard?" she asked.

"Sleeping." Holding open the heavy glass door, he allowed her to lead the way. Putting the guard to sleep had been a bit of a heavy lift, but a necessary one.

She crept forward, darting looks left and right, making him smile. Not bothering to hide the echo of his footfalls on the marble floor, he lagged just far enough behind to admire her sexy ass twitching as she took one cautious step after another. Past the teller stations with their antique wrought-iron cage fronts, down a short hall decorated with crown molding, and around a corner to the steel vault door.

Pausing, he asked, "I need to know how big the portal item is and what it's made of."

She looked at him, deep worry in her eyes.

He reached out, smoothed a hand over her cheek, and pulled her into a kiss. "It'll be fine. I'm going to create a crucible. All you have to do is drop the portal in."

"That's all?"

He nodded. "It'll melt the metal and ruin the crystalline structure that gives it power."

She took a shaky breath. "A gold pendant. About the size of a walnut." With a small voice, she added, "Please tell me this will work."

Her words touched him. He bent and kissed her again, gently, reverently. "I will never let you down."

Letting her go, he placed both hands on the wheel lock and twisted until there was a clunk. The door swung open silently. Inside, rows and rows of lockers lined the walls.

Tanika walked straight to the left wall and pulled out her key. "It also requires a bank manager key."

"Never mind. Just point me to the correct box."

She did, and he breathed a release spell at the lock. His heart was thundering in his ears. Everything hinged on getting this done before Elim realized what was happening. "You don't need your key. Be ready to open it. I'm going to conjure a crucible now."

Closing his eyes, he summoned the whirling pool of energy from the pit of his stomach and focused it at waist level in front of him. Heat filled the room, radiating outward from the glowing pinpoint floating there. Opening his eyes, he stared at the growing circle of light, willing it to become a tiny, blinding sun. He flicked a glance at Tanika and nodded, every ounce of his attention on the brewing heat.

Tanika yanked the box outward and fumbled with the flip-top lid. She pulled out a black velvet pouch and let the heavy box crash to the floor. He could feel the portal's energy, smell the anise-sweet scent of its magic.

But that magic no longer had any power over him. Ophir breathed through his nose, pouring all his strength into the crucible. Sustaining this much energy output could cause him to collapse. Tanika had to hurry. She struggled with the pouch's drawstring, and he shouted, "The whole thing."

Understanding lit her features, and she tossed the entire pouch into the whirling heat. The velvet went up in a puff of dark smoke. In the center of the crucible, the pendant darkened for an eye blink, glowed red, then golden white.

When he was sure the structure was melted through, Ophir cut the energy flow. The melted gold continued to hover a moment longer, still caught in the force of residual energy. Then it fell like a giant teardrop to the floor, landing with a splat.

Tanika jumped backward to avoid the volcano-hot spatter. Ophir stepped forward, worried she'd been burned. He might be immune to the heat, but he should have warned her. He'd taken no more than one step when his legs gave out and he fell face first onto the hard tile, the world going dark around him.

Tanika believed she was strong. A big girl. She ought to be able to drag a man across a perfectly flat, smooth floor. But no. Ophir's big frame might as well have been an elephant. Her ballet flats refused to find purchase on the highly-polished marble, and she was forced to remove them, praying the police couldn't ID a person from their toe prints.

Even in bare feet, it took her forever to slide him as far as the vault door. She paused to rest, staring into the room of safe deposit boxes. Globs of hardened gold adhered to the marble, and a crack marred the tile her metal box had hit. The box's lid was bent, but she'd managed to force it back into its slot while waiting for Ophir to regain consciousness. When he didn't, she'd had no choice but to move him herself.

She knelt next to him, smoothing her fingertips over his brows. She hadn't thought a djinn could be rendered unconscious. Was mortality already creeping up on him? Her stomach churned with regret. He was hers, and now it was her turn to take care of him. They had to get out of here before the bank opened in...she glanced at her phone. Forty minutes. *Shit!* She grabbed his wrist and pulled again, inching him along the floor until he cleared the vault's threshold.

Stepping over him, she moved his legs aside and pushed the heavy metal door shut, spinning the locking wheel. What would the employees think when they got here? She shook her head. She had to trust Ophir could cover their tracks—was somehow *still* covering their tracks. At least there'd been no alarms so far.

Grabbing his wrist, she pulled again, progressing to the corner of the short hall leading to the main lobby. Ophir's hip snagged on the corner as she attempted to round it, and she had to tear his belt loop free of where it had caught on the baseboard's ornate brass corner plate. *Stupid, fancy bank.*

Sweat trickled between her shoulder blades. She tugged harder, all too aware of the ticking clock echoing in the lobby. Someone would be arriving to open the bank at any moment. Dropping to her knees next to

Ophir, she patted his cheeks. "Ophir, wake up." She smacked him harder. "Wake up!"

His eyes rolled beneath his lids. Then his lashes parted the barest millimeter. He mumbled something unintelligible.

"We have to get out of here. The bank's about to open, and I can't drag you the rest of the way fast enough."

A shiver rippled along his skin and seemed to reach into his bones. Then he rolled to his side, pushing upright on wobbly feet. Relief made her own knees weak. She wedged one shoulder under Ophir's arm and led him toward the doors. Down the steps. Into the bright morning sun.

Across the street, a man jogged behind his leashed dog. A pickup truck zipped past, country music twanging from the open windows. No one seemed to take any notice of two people limping across the empty parking lot.

Cursing her choice of parking spot, she helped Ophir limp across the vast stretch of pavement to the convertible. The top was up, and she frowned, not remembering Ophir putting it up. But she'd been so frightened, he could have walked on his hands into the bank and she might not have noticed such a detail. As they neared the car, the soft top accordioned back, exposing the interior.

Elim sat in the driver's seat.

anika let out a half scream, and Ophir nearly fell at the sudden loss of her support. He forced his bleary eyes to focus, catching himself with one hand on the top edge of the convertible's windshield. Tanika was repeating, "No, no, no..."

Elim grinned at him from behind the steering wheel, his perfect white teeth as menacing as fangs. His face had lost its craggy lines, and the subtle fire in the depths of his eyes glowed with djinn health. "Where are we going next?"

Ophir somehow found the strength to straighten, glaring down at the djinn. "How the hell are you here?" He'd felt no flow of magic from the portal between the time it had emerged from the box until the crucible rendered it useless. "This shouldn't be possible."

"My dear mistress's stubbornness taught me a few things." Elim leered at Tanika. "One of which being that I no longer need a portal to move between realms."

Still reeling from energy depletion, Ophir tried to focus. He'd known the crucible would cost him, but he'd counted on not needing much magic immediately after finishing the job. And never considered he'd pass out completely. Poor Tanika'd dragged him out all on her own. He turned to her. "Are you okay?"

Her lips were still formed around the word "no" and her skin was ashen. "You promised he'd be trapped on the other side."

Guilt gnawed at his chest. "He should be. I don't understand." His guilt turned to anger, giving him strength. He squared his shoulders and faced Elim. "How are you doing this?"

Like a racecar driver, Elim lifted himself up and swung his legs over the car's door, keeping the vehicle between himself and Ophir. But he didn't act afraid. Instead, he pushed his shoulders back and shook his head as if enjoying a sea breeze. "The tiniest connection to an Earth-bound djinn is enough of an anchor, it seems."

Outrage filled Ophir. He hadn't felt any shifting of

power, but this method of travel between dimensions was new to him. "You're using *me*?"

Tanika sank to her knees on the pavement.

"I wonder what my range will be?" Elim turned his back and took a few steps away from the car.

Tanika started sobbing.

Ophir stalked around the hood, his legs protesting the movement. He needed to come up with another deal, and fast. "Wait. I have questions."

Elim paused and looked over his shoulder, a slight smile on his lips. "What do you offer for answers?"

Dammit, he wasn't ready for this. Not mentally or physically. If he only had something—anything—to use as leverage. Stopping his advance, he stared intently at the djinn. "Do you have access to full power?"

Laughing, Elim faced away and resumed walking. "The wish has released me. Now, if you'll excuse me, I believe the police have arrived, and I don't want to be caught up in your mess. I have quite a few lost years to make up for."

Elim winked out of existence as flashing lights appeared at the end of the street, headed in the bank's direction.

Ophir wobbled back toward Tanika and pulled her toward the car. His glamour would make police look the other way—a useful spell for driving, and doubly useful now. He expended a tiny fragment of energy to strengthen the magic, fighting the nausea that swept in as a result. Was his extraordinary weakness from more than just creating the crucible? He'd have to think on that, but later. He shoved Tanika into the passenger side door just as a police car squealed to a halt at the bank's front steps. The rumpled guard greeted the officers at the glass door.

Ophir sagged in the driver's seat, Tanika equally wilted in the passenger seat. He closed his eyes and let his head fall back against the headrest. "That went horribly wrong. I'm so sorry, Tanika."

Her shaking breath suddenly huffed to anger, and she began beating his shoulder with her fists. "You said he wouldn't be able to come back!"

"I had no way of knowing." His heart broke as he realized how badly he'd betrayed her. How much he'd underestimated Elim's power. He grabbed her fists, self-recriminations making him feel like he weighed a thousand pounds. Love had made him impulsive. Reckless. He should've thought his plan through better. After essentially losing his portal, Elim had used Tanika's unfulfilled wish to access Earth, so it should be no surprise he could find yet another thread to follow. A thread Ophir provided. Ophir swallowed, an idea forming. A horrific idea, but one that should work, using the only leverage Elim had provided.

He hugged Tanika's balled fists against his heart. "I believe we can still banish Elim from this world."

She stared at him, her breasts heaving, tears coating her cheeks. "How?"

He pressed his lips together, hesitant to speak the solution aloud. A solution that would finally grant him his eight-hundred-year-old wish. The wish he no longer wanted. "If I go back, he no longer has a channel."

Her mouth fell open. "You can't! You said you'd stay with me forever!"

"I know." He stared sightlessly out the windshield. Every molecule in his body ached at the thought of leaving her. "But we can't allow him to stay."

In the rearview mirror, he spotted a police officer squinting the convertible's direction. Dammit, their suspicion was too strong. Even the glamour could only hold up against certain levels of attention. Elim was probably watching from some nearby tree and laughing. Grinding his teeth, Ophir started the engine, slammed the car into drive, and peeled out, tearing up an edge of the grass between the sidewalk and street. As soon as he was several blocks away, he slowed again and pulled into an empty driveway.

Turning to him with knit brows, Tanika said, "I see a

major problem. Didn't you say you needed a portal? You can't go back without one."

He'd considered this when he first decided on this course. "The weakness I experienced is due to more than merely creating the crucible. I think it's because of Elim. He used me as an anchor between Earth and our realm. I should be able to trace the path back to the source. Back to... home." The word felt like poison on his tongue.

Still barefoot, Tanika jumped out of the car and started walking. He climbed out after her and jogged to catch up. "Where are you going?"

"I don't know. I just want it all to go away."

He stopped, letting her pull ahead. "I promised you I'd free Earth of his presence. And I mean to do it."

Her steps faltered and her shoulders slumped. "It's not fair. I only just found you."

In three strides he was next to her, his heart in full agreement. Yet he couldn't stay here with her, not with a potentially vengeful djinn stalking her. The only way to protect both her and the rest of humanity was to go back. "I have to do this. He's a danger to you and every other person he meets."

"Isn't there another way? Would a wish break the connection?" She looked at him with hopeful eyes.

He shook his head. "We're immune to each other's magic, remember?"

She shoved both palms ineffectually against his chest. "I don't want to have to choose between you and him! I lose no matter what!"

He opened his arms, relieved when she fell into them, pressing her cheek hard against his chest. Resting his chin atop her head, he breathed deeply of her sweet anise and citrus scent. "I'm so sorry."

There was really nothing more to say. So he held her while she cried. He looked at the achingly blue sky overhead, took a deep breath of the morning breeze, full of the scent of cooking bacon and the rose bushes climbing a trellis on a nearby house. Ran his palms along Tanika's bare arms, enjoying the velvet skin beneath his touch. All these things he would lose when he once again became pure spirit.

She turned her chin to look up into his face. "There's no other choice. You have to go, don't you?"

He nodded, and brushed his lips gently against hers. Her beautiful face crumpled into tears once again, and he crushed her tightly against him, never wanting to let her go. The world seemed to stand still around them, time losing all meaning, and yet barely any time at all passed. He would hold this in his memory for all eternity. Finally, he pushed her away, holding lightly to her arms.

"Now?" She whispered.

He wiped moisture from beneath her eye with a thumb and put it to his lips, tasting salt. Even the sad things he'd miss. "Before he has a chance to trick another soul."

She stepped back, body rigid, eyes tight. The tendons on her neck stood out with repressed tears. Holding up her right hand, she regarded the palm. "I only have one heart line. Unbroken." She held it out for him to see. "I love you, Ophir. I will until the end of my days."

His chest was so tight, he wondered if it might not be possible to die right then and there. "And I will love you through all eternity."

With that, he closed his eyes and focused on the tiny thread he now knew had always been there. The one that allowed him to do small magic, yet had never seemed large enough to allow a soul to pass. He pulled deep from what little energy remained within him, feeling for the djinn in his realm to anchor him, as Elim had suggested. There were plenty there to choose from. He stretched himself thinner than he ever thought possible, felt his cells vibrate, his molecules dissolve... and his consciousness become energy.

Tanika stared at the spot Ophir had stood only moments before. She'd seen her djinn dematerialize a million times. It had always been a relief. Now, watching Ophir fade from existence, it felt like the world had cracked in two, leaving nothing but an empty shell. She stared at her palm again. The strong and unbroken heart line. The lifeline following the long curve of her thumb.

She walked to the car and climbed in, numb. Drove back to the salon without knowing quite how she got there. The security gate moved aside without complaint, as if sensing her inability to argue. Inside the familiar, dark space, she paused, staring into nothingness.

What was she doing? What could she do? Her life had no meaning left. No wish to live for. No wish to live *against.* Elim was gone. Ophir was gone. Her purpose was gone. Sure, she had an awesome new car, but it meant little to her without the sexy man who drove it.

Still in the dark, she flopped into her chair, staring at her shadowy outline in the mirror. Her wish had been granted. But not fulfilled. Didn't that mean something? Didn't Elim still owe her?

Some spark deep inside her ignited, like a fire against her breastbone. Narrowing her eyes she glowered at her reflection. Two pinpricks of lavender light had her spinning the chair around to look behind her. "Hello?"

Her heartbeat thundered in her ears. Rising, she scurried to the light switch and flooded the room. She was alone. She looked at the mirror again. Her grief-stricken eyes stared back. She must have been imagining things.

Shaking her head until her brain rattled, she decided to ready the shop for opening. It was all she had left. She wondered if Elim's horrible spell still tarnished the place, and looked hard at the folding chairs near the darkened window and the shabby velvet curtain in the back. She'd never seen the taint, so she wasn't sure why she expected to see it now. Well, if nothing else, she could try a cleansing, just to be sure.

By the time Birdie arrived several hours later, Tanika was airing out the last of the sage smudge and hand-scrubbing the floor. Birdie had to raise her voice to be heard above the Zen piano concerto playing loudly from Tanika's phone. "I know you're an early riser, but this is going a little overboard, even for you."

Tanika sat up on her knees and wiped an errant curl from her cheek with the back of her forearm. She didn't feel any better. All she could think about was finding a way to reach Ophir. A seance. A lucid dream. There had to be a way. "We needed cleansing."

"If you say so." Birdie clicked over the newly clean floor in her kitten heels and stopped the music. "This have anything to do with your date last night?"

Last night? Had it only been one day since she'd met Ophir? How could so much have happened? She felt like she'd been struck by lightning, and every emotion had been seared to ash. She dropped back to all fours and resumed scrubbing. "I found my soul mate."

Birdie gasped and rushed over, slapping Tanika's shoulder. "Get out. Your soul mate?" When Tanika kept scrubbing, she bent and snatched the sponge away. "Up. Now."

Unable to summon the will to fight, Tanika rose and stumbled to her chair, her knees aching and damp. Once again she flopped, this time not facing the mirror. Birdie fisted one hand on a hip and raised both brows. "You don't drop a bombshell like finding a soul mate and then say nothing else. Now tell."

Tanika shook her head. Birdie would never believe the truth. Yet a lie was an impossible task. "He can't be part of my world. So he left."

Birdie's mouth hung open in shock. "He left? You let him leave? Why?" Her gaze narrowed. "Is it because he was loaded?" She walked over and spun Tanika's chair to face her own, then plopped down to look at her. "Did he leave you, or did you leave him?"

The barrage of questions would normally have made Tanika laugh. Today, it only made her jaw quiver, and her chest grow tight.

"Oh, girl, I'm sorry." Birdie jumped up and raced over to pull Tanika's shoulders into a hug. "I shouldn't be so nosy."

"It's okay." Tanika sniffed, leaning her head against her friend's comforting warmth. "Everything is just too complicated to explain."

"Why don't I do your hair? You seem like you could use a little pampering."

Tanika nodded. Perhaps some physical comfort would help relieve her ache. At this point she hadn't much else left. She rose and followed Birdie to the wash sink, leaning her head back and allowing the hot water to soak into her scalp. Birdie's fingers massaged fragrant suds into her curls, and Tanika closed her eyes, allowing tears to leak toward her hairline. If Birdie noticed, she didn't say anything, just hummed under her breath and continued scrubbing.

The spray of rinse water was a blessed white noise Tanika found surprisingly soothing. Hypnotic. Birdie wrung her hair, and worked conditioner into the ends.

The salon bell jangled, and Birdie's fingers paused a moment. "I'll be right with you!"

Her bright voice jarred Tanika from semi-meditation. "Thank you, Birdie. I can finish myself. Go take care of our client."

"I can wait." A man's voice said.

Tanika's entire body tightened. She bolted upright in the chair, blinking runnels of water from her eyes. Standing just inside the open doorway was Elim.

Her words choked her, filled her throat and cut off her air without emitting a sound. She clutched her middle. How could he be here?

Elim glanced her up and down as if she was inconsequential, then turned his brilliant smile toward Birdie, one hand extended as if to shake. "You must be Birdie. I've been dying to meet you."

"No!" Tanika shot from the chair, intercepting his outstretched hand and smacking it aside. She rounded on Birdie. "Leave. Immediately."

Birdie's face paled with shock. "Is everything all right?"

"Please, Birdie. No questions. Just go."

Gaze darting between Tanika and Elim, Birdie scurried past. "Should I call the police?"

"No. Just get away from here as fast as you can. Far away. Don't come back until I call you."

Birdie fled.

Tanika squared her shoulders and advanced on Elim until she was nose to chest, looking up into his face. "How the hell are you doing this?"

"You thought my connection to Earth was through Ophir?" He clucked his tongue and turned away from her, surveying the salon as if seeing it for the first time. "You cleansed in here. I wondered if you'd ever notice."

"You said your connection to another djinn gave you a portal."

"No, I said my connection to djinn blood was enough for a portal."

Her stomach fell. Djinn blood. Ophir had believed she might have a trace within her. "He went back for nothing?" Her words scratched from her throat.

"Oh, my poor Tanika. So lost without a man."

Her cheek twitched, and the fire she'd felt earlier against her breastbone blossomed once again. "I'm lost without my *soul mate*." She stalked toward him once again, punching a finger into his chest with each word. "You owe me a wish."

His face paled. "Now slow down. You—"

"My wish was for a mate."

He back pedaled, holding both hands up, palm out. "I'll find you a new one. Just give me some time."

"I already have a mate. A mate for eternity. What I don't have is my happily-ever-after." A sudden realization hit her. He *couldn't* fulfill his end of the bargain. Ophir was immune to his spells. What did that mean in the world of djinn, with their rules about truth and deal brokering? "You took your payment up front. And now I'm calling your deal."

"I can show him how to come back."

"He won't. We decided it was more important to be rid of you than it was to stay together. As long as you're alive, we'll deny ourselves." She crossed her arms, her victory a bittersweet bile in her throat. "I think the term in chess is checkmate."

Two overhead lights shattered, and he swelled like he had so many times in the past to intimidate her. "I didn't have to show myself to you. My range is quite far, now. I only returned to be sure you were all right."

"You returned to gloat," she gritted between clenched teeth. "And I want my wish."

His figure began to shimmer, the purple spark in his

eyes guttering like a candle at the end of its wick. "You can't. Tanika, I beg of you. You don't understand."

"I'd ask you to bring back Mom and Grandma, but you can't revive the dead. So there's no way for you to repay your debt to me except with your life." She bared her teeth at him. "I want it. Now."

His eyes grew wide, the flame shrinking to minuscule pinpricks. He shook his head and opened his mouth, but no sound emerged. Instead, the oval formed by his lips grew. And grew. Impossibly huge, it consumed his face. Opened into a pit of nothingness before her eyes, as if he was swallowing his own body backwards. Larger and larger the oval grew, drawing him in, shrinking him. Swallowing him. Sucking down with a whoosh into a florescent purple globe of light.

It hovered there, the flames within it flaring and swirling in patterns like galaxies being born. She stepped closer, mesmerized. She'd won?

The globe shot forward into the burning spot in her chest, slamming her backward to the cold, hard floor.

Tanika woke to gentle fingers on her brow. Without opening her eyes, she assessed every square inch of her body. Every nerve tingled, and she could feel the blood coursing through her veins. Breathing was a magnificent experience, the sweet licorice scent of anise filling her nose. She opened her eyes to meet a chocolate brown gaze.

Ophir's face spread into a grin. "Wake up, my love."

She sucked in a breath. Blinked. Reached a hand up to trace the hard line of his jaw. Solid. Warm. Her head was cradled in his lap, and the salon's flickering florescent bulbs backlit his hair like a halo. "Am I dreaming?"

"If you are, then so am I." He gently slid from beneath her and rose, holding a hand down to help her up. "Are you well enough to stand?"

Gripping his hand, she stood. Easily. Lightly. She felt more alive than she'd ever thought possible. "I'm... confused."

Ophir pulled her close, enveloping her. "Oh, my brilliant Tanika. You don't know what you've done."

She shook her head, wrapping her arms tightly around his solid waist. "I really don't. Please explain?"

A chuckle rumbled through his chest, filling her with joy. If this was death, it was the happiest thing that had ever happened to her. He kissed her hair, then her forehead, then pressed his mouth close to her ear. "You caught Elim in the bargain of bargains. An impossible debt." He pulled away just far enough to look down into her face. "A debt that could only be repaid with every ounce of his being. You are now immortal, my lovely bride."

Her legs suddenly refused to hold her, but Ophir was there. Catching her, he carried her to her salon chair and set her down. She stammered, "Immortal? What does that mean?"

"We can be together for eternity."

The hope swelling her heart threatened to burst. She shook her head, sure she must be dreaming. Or dead. "I thought no wish could ever make me immortal."

"A regular wish couldn't." He grinned at her. "A human soul doesn't carry enough energy for such a wish. But the soul of a djinn is a different matter."

The memory of that purple globe embedding itself within her rocked her again. She shook her head in disbelief. "He gave me his immortality?"

Ophir nodded. "Not gave, exactly. More like made restitution. It was the only way he could fulfill his bargain."

Tears overwhelmed her, and she buried her face in her hands. "I can't believe it."

He cupped her head with both hands, showering kisses over her hair and the hands covering her face until she lowered them and accepted his touch on her eyelids, cheeks, and lips. He breathed against her, a life-giving sensation. Grabbing handfuls of his shirt, she pulled him closer, kissing him for real. Lips hungry against his as if this one kiss had to last forever.

After a long moment, she pulled away. "But how are you here?"

"Our mate bond drew me as surely as any portal."

When he said it, she felt the connection between them, like an unbreakable ribbon around her heart. "Bound." Excitement made her nervous. Unsure where to look or what to do. She had her happily-ever-after? For real? "Can we have children?"

"Of course." He smirked. "But one thing at a time, my love. We have a very long honeymoon to enjoy first."

The jangle of the shop's door drew Tanika's attention. Birdie burst into the salon with Mr. Daniels and a police officer close behind. Birdie stopped short, her brows knit as she took in Ophir kneeling next to the salon chair. "Oh!"

The police officer moved into the room, looking around with a concerned eye. Tanika felt a shimmer of magic ripple from Ophir. The tension in the room relaxed. Mr. Daniels winked and said, "Glad to see you two lovebirds getting along." With that, he left.

Tipping his hat, the police man left as well.

Birdie wiped a tear from the corner of her eye and

fanned herself. "Oh. My. God. I knew he was meant for you the moment I saw him."

Tanika nudged Ophir. "Don't do that to her."

"Do what?"

"Make her all gushy."

He laughed and rose from his knees. "I'm not, believe me. Birdie is gushy all on her own."

One hand fluttering over her heart, Birdie rushed to the chair across from where Tanika sat. "You two are perfect together, just like I thought." She settled into her chair and looked expectantly between them. "I want to hear the whole thing, from start to finish. A love story right here in our Seance Salon."

Tanika beamed at Ophir, her heart light as she thought about their future. Their very long future. "There's really not much to say. He came back for me. That's all that matters."

Ophir smiled back. "Soul mates are meant to be together, bound for eternity."

Tanika threaded her fingers into Ophir's, the chaste touch warming her as surely as his fiery kisses. "I'm so glad you found our little salon."

"And I'm so happy to have finally found home."

Happiness surrounded her like she'd never imagined possible.

Tanika smiled as Birdie made another silly face, and the chubby toddler she held up to the mirror bubbled with laughter. Tiny handprints marred the glass along with a few slobbery spots where Theon had kissed himself. He was the spitting image of Ophir, with dark hair, fathomless coffee-brown eyes, and even the hint of a dimple at the edge of his mouth. And if Birdie was any indication, he was already killing it with the ladies.

"Come on, Theon." Tanika reached for her son. "Aunt Birdie has work to do."

"I'm never too busy to spend time with this little cutie." Birdie blew a raspberry against the boy's cheek before releasing him to Tanika's grasp. "You don't bring him around enough these days."

"I'll try to be better." Theon's weight settled into Tanika's arms and his familiar, sweet-baby scent filled her with joy. He flung his arms around her neck and gave her an open-mouthed kiss on her cheek, and the woman getting her hair cut at the station beside Birdie's cooed in appreciation.

The salon buzzed with activity, thriving since the glamour Elim had placed over it had been removed. The once tiny shop now took up most of the block and had fourteen hair stations as well as a spa section in the back. Birdie ran everything almost single-handedly, allowing Tanika to focus on her new family. Tanika only came in to give an occasional psychic reading with one of her old clients. It was too bad her absorption of Elim's power hadn't given her a djinn's ability to grant wishes, but that didn't mean her previous ability to read auras was any less real. She often wondered when and if Theon would develop powers, and if they'd be like hers or more substantial like his father's; Ophir said the child might not develop powers at all.

Shifting Theon's weight to one hip, Tanika looked her petite friend up and down, noting how thin she looked. "You should take a vacation."

"Soon as I find a hot guy like Ophir to rub me down with sunscreen." Birdie winked.

Tanika flushed, the vivid memory of her most recent

trip to a remote beach with Ophir washing through her. There were definite perks to being married to a guy who could snap his fingers and take you anywhere in the world at any time.

The phone rang, and Tanika waved goodbye as Birdie picked it up. Ophir was at the cafe, probably glutting himself on pastries. She stepped out onto the sidewalk and hurried toward the scent of cinnamon, sugar, and chocolate.

Ophir met her part way, a large, bright pink box in hand. "All done?"

Theon squealed and reached for his father. Ophir traded Tanika the box for the the child and settled Theon comfortably in the crook of an arm. She loved seeing the two of them together.

"Open that." He nodded at the box. "Mr. Daniels had a big selection today."

She lifted the lid, the aroma of buttery sweet goodness rising from inside. An assortment of doughnuts, brownies, big soft cookies, and two eclairs were arranged in pretty papers. She picked through the delectable treats as Ophir carried Theon to the car and settled him into his car seat. Although Ophir could take them anywhere and give them anything, they mostly lived a regular human life.

And she loved every minute of it.

Finally settling on a brownie, she sank her teeth into the creamy, ganache coating, flooding her tongue with dark chocolate. She gave a groan of dramatic pleasure.

Theon stretched a hand out, making grabby motions toward the treat. Ophir plucked a cream-filled doughnut from the open box, handing it to the child. Whether Theon ever developed powers or not, he obviously had full control over Ophir's heart.

With his chubby fists clamped around the doughnut, Theon smashed it against his open mouth, spewing Bavarian cream down his front.

"You're giving him that whole thing?" Tanika said around a mouthful of chocolate. "That's going to be terrible to clean up."

Ophir smirked and snapped his fingers, making the dribbles vanish. Then he closed the car door and turned to pull her into his arms, leaning backward against the windows.

She settled against his hard chest and tilted her face up to his with a smile. "Cheater."

In the reflection of the car's windows, she watched a group of young women pass by on the sidewalk behind her, gazes fixed with longing on her and Ophir. She took a deep breath of contentment. *My days of longing are over*. Who would've ever guessed her wish could turn out this way?

Using the pad of one thumb, Ophir wiped frosting from the corner of her mouth. "You're almost as bad as Theon."

She caught his hand and licked the frosting clean. His eyes darkened with desire. Without breaking his gaze, she sucked the digit into her mouth, twirling her tongue around it suggestively. Between their bodies, his erection surged to life, and a matching heat grew between her thighs.

He made a low sound in his chest. "I think I've been a bad influence on you."

Tanika smiled around his thumb and released it, kissing the tip one last time. "I think I like having a genie at my beck and call."

He wrapped an arm around her lower back and pulled her closer. "Your wish is my command, my love."

Lowering his head, he claimed her mouth with his. The kiss flooded her with more than desire. It filled her with happiness. Contentment. Love. She'd finally reached her happily ever after. And she was ready for eternity together.

Dear Reader,

Thank you for reading The Djinn's Desire. Craving more sweet and steamy paranormal romance? You'll love my Alaska Alphas series because it features characters you'll fall in love with. Book one, Untamed Instinct, starts with an outcast shifter who wanders the Alaskan wilderness alone—until he saves a witch's life. Can their forbidden love find a happily ever after?

Tap the cover to buy now or keep reading for a sneak peek!

P.S. Want to stay in touch? Sign up for my VIP newsletter. Members get exclusive giveaways, sneak

peeks of future books, and bonus scenes. There's an exclusive deleted prologue from The Djinn's Desire *waiting for you right now!*

SIGN UP FOR TAMSIN'S NEWSLETTER:
https://bookhip.com/TXBMPB

UNTAMED INSTINCT

SNEAK PEEK

Adrian crouched among the cottonwood leaves, claws digging into the bark as he surveyed the dead moose in the clearing below. He'd been waiting here in his mountain lion form for several hours and was eager to move on, but had to be certain the carcass had been deserted before he drew closer to investigate. He'd received numerous reports of abandoned animal kills over the last few weeks, and his supervisor at the ranger station wanted whoever—or whatever—was doing the poaching to be tracked down.

Scattered throughout the Wrangell-St. Elias Park, the previous sites had been old before Adrian reached them, the evidence around the carcasses obscured by smaller predators and decay. This site seemed fresher, the stench of rot less intense, although flies swarmed over the bull's hide and stubby, velvet-covered antlers. If the killer was human, they weren't out for trophies. And they definitely weren't doing it for meat. Someone or something was killing for fun, and they were slowly moving closer to human-occupied lands.

Adrian's tail twitched angrily, and he let out a grunt of resignation before dropping nimbly to the ground. The scent of rotting flesh grew stronger as he approached, and flies rose in a cloud, exposing gashes writhing with fresh maggots.

He circled the moose, estimating it had been dead slightly longer than twenty-four hours. Clawed paw prints, almost twice the size of his own, scarred the earth around the kill. He lowered his muzzle and sniffed, tail lashing. The familiar musk of a grizzly filled his nose. *Shifter grizzly*. He released a hiss of displeasure. The last thing the shifter community wanted was a rogue member drawing attention to the national park. Randall, Adrian's tough-as-nails wolf supervisor, would not like this.

Fuck, Adrian didn't like it either. Mountain lions weren't unheard of in Alaska, but rare enough to cause a ruckus among humans if sighted. The vast wilds of the park were his refuge—his *territory* in the mind of his mountain lion. The local bear shifters would want to take care of a rogue grizzly themselves.

Adrian exposed his canines and turned away, prowling through the trees toward his ranger cabin to call his supervisor.

Just out of sight of his cabin, he shifted and retrieved the uniform he kept in a hollow tree, shrugging into his clothing before emerging into the clearing. His cabin was a small log building nestled next to one of the many rock faces jutting from the mountain, roof covered in thick moss and a small porch screened in from mosquitoes. One of the more popular trailheads started nearby, and a small message board fluttered with notices campers left to each other at the end of his overgrown driveway.

Inside the two-room cabin, a few small windows shed dusky light over the sparse furnishings. Passing the small front area with a table, a propane fridge, a wood stove, and an old sofa, he moved to the bedroom where a king-sized bed took up almost every inch of space. He retrieved his cell phone from the nightstand and moved to the corner of the front room where he got the best reception. He kept an old ham radio in the shed for when the notoriously spotty cell service didn't work, but he couldn't talk to Randall about shifter business over the radio. Thankfully, the phone showed two bars today. He dialed the main ranger office.

"This is HQ," a woman's nasal voice answered.

"Cherry, it's Adrian. I need to talk to Randall."

"Oh, hi, handsome!" Her voice brightened. "We haven't heard from you in a while. How've you been?"

Adrian bared his teeth and reminded himself to be polite; Cherry was human. "Doing fine."

He hated social niceties, which was why he'd become a ranger in the first place. This remote location suited him well, and he only ventured into town when he needed supplies. Most of his duties allowed him to patrol the trails alone, talking to the occasional hiker and reporting any problems. Several times a year he had to oversee search and rescue operations when a hiker got lost, but more often than not, he found the missing person before a full team even arrived.

"You doing okay on handouts?" Cherry chirped back.

He glanced toward the door where a stack of papers had gathered a layer of dust. He was supposed to pass them out to tourists, but since he avoided people, he used very few. "All good. I just need to talk to Randall."

"You betcha."

The phone clicked. A few heartbeats later, the supervisor's voice came on the line. "Adrian, what's up?"

"I've got a lead on the poacher. I found a spike-fork moose abandoned yesterday, and there's fresh grizzly sign all over the place. Smells like a shifter."

"Shit. Don't tell me the infection's moved to our territory."

"What infection?"

"Rogues." The sound of fingernails against beard stubble scratched over the phone line. "Two rogue wolves and a moose were put down in Anchorage over the winter, then a black bear outside Valdez this spring. No rhyme or reason to why. Council sent out a memo a while back. Don't you read your emails, Adrian?"

Adrian glanced at the dust-covered laptop under the nightstand. "Not like I have wifi out here, Randall. I'll catch up next time I go into town."

Randall made a frustrated noise over the phone. "Well, if a shifter's behind these abandoned kills, it's likely a rogue. File your report then go handle it ASAP."

"Me? Isn't this Den business?" Although the Council oversaw shifter law, local shifter groups liked to take care of their own business.

"Not this time. A travel blogger already posted about the kills. We need to get ahead of the news before it goes viral. Take your rifle."

"I'm a ranger, not a SWAT team, Randall."

"This is your territory. I need you to handle it. There could be hikers in danger."

"Fuck." Adrian grimaced. "What if he shifts before he dies?" It was one thing for a ranger to take down a dangerous bear. Quite another if a human body showed up killed by a ranger's bullet. And in a face-to-face fight, a mountain lion couldn't stand up to a full-grown grizzly, especially a shifter gone rogue.

"Make your first shot count."

"I hate this shit." Hanging up, Adrian pocketed his phone and grabbed his rifle before heading back outside. He'd file a report when he got back. Best to get on the trail while it was still relatively warm.

He started up his ATV, its disused engine letting out a disgusting belch of smoke. The damn thing cut off his ability to hear or smell anything, which made his mountain lion bristle in discomfort. *I know, me too.* But he couldn't carry his rifle while in feline form.

Stowing the weapon in the mounted case on the front of the ATV, he rolled out of the cabin's clearing toward the trailhead parking lot.

CHAPTER TWO

Darcy stopped her Subaru and eyed the overgrown path. According to Google, this dirt road should lead to a trailhead parking lot, but it looked like if she drove any farther, she might end up "parked" more permanently. Her all-wheel drive had managed the old, rutted road, but the path was getting narrower, with branches rubbing her door panels. *Did I take a wrong turn?*

She glanced in her rearview mirror. There had been a space wide enough to turn around a short way back. Putting the car in reverse, she carefully maneuvered through the brush, backing into a flat area that looked like it would make a nice campsite.

The overcast sky filtered dimly through the thick canopy of trees, and she hadn't seen a soul since turning into what had started out as a fairly decent dirt road. She rolled down her window and breathed in the verdant forest air. *This looks like as good a place to start as any.*

Her interview with the coven was the day after tomorrow, and she'd come in search of herbs to make an eloquence potion. This would be her last-ditch effort to overcome the stutter that ruined every spell she tried to cast. Poor Aunt Willow still had a patch of white hair behind one ear from one of her lessons. Darcy'd tried to buy an eloquence potion from the local apothecary shop, but it turned out it only worked for the person who made it, and the effects would not be permanent. But she didn't need to be *good* at incantations, only steady enough to pass the coven's apprenticeship test.

Cutting the engine, she reached over to the passenger seat to retrieve her copy of *Wild Edible and Medicinal Plants of the Pacific Northwest*. She was more familiar with gardens than wilderness, but her mom had sent her to summer camp every year of her childhood, and the forest didn't daunt her.

Tapping her phone, she opened her GPS app and pinned her current location so she could find her way back, then tucked it and the book into a reusable grocery bag alongside a small trowel, a pair of purple and yellow gardening gloves, and a compact rain poncho. She looked around as she stepped out of the car, taking in a circle of stones around an overgrown fire pit. The mossy log seats around it obviously hadn't been disturbed in quite a while, and knee-high saplings and brush filled the clearing.

Locking the car even though she doubted she needed to, she headed toward what looked like a trail on the uphill side of the clearing. According to her book, wild rhodiola rosea grew on rocky slopes at high altitudes.

She set off between the trees, scanning the surrounding plants for signs of fleshy rhodiola leaves. A thick layer of dry leaves and twigs crunched under her feet, birds sang overhead, and in the distance a woodpecker tatted out a rhythm. She let out a contented sigh, running her fingertips over the smooth gray trunk of a quaking aspen as she passed.

A scraggly thicket of salmonberries crowded the

trail, and she sampled a few, letting the sweet juice coat her tongue. A mosquito buzzed her ear, and she reached into her bag for her homemade insect repellant. She wasn't yet much good at magical potions, but she had a decent grasp of essential oils, and her minty-citrus concoction not only worked, it smelled good. After dousing herself, she tucked the small spray bottle away and continued on.

The path grew steeper, making her calves burn as she climbed until she reached a sharp turn. To her right, the trail paralleled the top of a rocky ridge, but about fifteen feet below, she spotted a clump of rosette shaped leaves. *Rhodiola?* She stepped toward the edge to get a better look.

The ground beneath her feet collapsed. Too startled to even scream, she bumped and slithered helplessly down the incline on her backside, coming to a stop among a rain of pebbles and dust.

More stunned than hurt, she sat up and pushed her strawberry blonde hair out of her face before struggling to her feet. Other than a few scrapes and a racing heartbeat, she wasn't hurt, thank the Goddess. Next to her, scaly rosettes of rhodiola crouched staunchly among the rocks. Amidst the dust, her minty-citrus scented insect repellant had become cloying. She pulled the crushed bottle from her bag and wrinkled her nose. Oily residue covered everything inside. She wiped her phone and the book on the leg of her jeans. At least she'd be insect-free for a while.

Along the cliff face behind her, a scoured swath of dirt and stone showed her path down the steep incline. It was a wonder she wasn't seriously injured. She peered both directions along the wall. Not one spot looked possible to climb.

"Fuck," she muttered. Her stutter never affected her curse words.

She turned back to the rhodiola. *Might as well make the most of the situation before I try to climb back up.* She pulled out her book to make sure the photos matched, then put on her gardening gloves and shoved a clump aside to get at the root. The plant seemed to grow directly from a crack in one of the large stones. If she could've used store-bought herbs, she would've, but for this potion, the rhodiola root had to be freshly gathered within seventy-two hours after a full moon.

Jabbing the pointed end of her trowel into the crack, she tried to pry it apart, but the tool scraped uselessly against the stone. She tried several angles, but the ground refused to give up its hold on the plant. Standing upright, she glared toward the overcast sky in frustration.

As if the heavens were laughing at her, a fat raindrop hit her square on the forehead. *Great.*

She wiped at the moisture with the back of one wrist, moving on to another nearby plant. All she succeeded in doing was breaking a fingernail down to the quick and snapping a few stems off at ground level. "I need these damn roots."

How could this be so hard? Her trowel didn't give her enough leverage against the rocks. She would have to come back with a full-sized shovel and try again. At least she knew where the rhodiola was now.

Stuffing her trowel and gloves back into her bag, she pulled out her phone to mark the spot on her app.

No reception.

She held the phone overhead and paced a few feet in either direction, waiting for a signal. The app refused to come up. Maybe the rock wall was blocking her. *God, what a day.*

Well, as long as she didn't stray from the wall, she wouldn't end up walking in circles. Eventually, she'd get reception again. Or at least find a relatively easy spot to climb and get back to the trail.

Phone in hand, she began walking along the base of the cliff.

CHAPTER THREE

Adrian stopped his ATV next to a blue Subaru Forester and cut the engine. What was a car doing so far off the road? He dismounted and circled the vehicle. Judging by the tire tracks, it'd only been here a few hours. A single set of footprints—a woman's, he'd guess by the size—headed straight toward a game trail that led to the moose kill site. He'd need to hurry if he wanted to catch her before she reached it.

He shouldered his rifle and started off, yearning for the ease of his mountain lion form. Where the trail veered to follow a ridge, a swath of fresh dirt marred the edge. Cautious of an undercut, he edged closer and peered over the drop-off. That landslide was definitely not the product of a controlled descent, but he didn't see a body. He called out, "Hello, anyone down there?"

Only wind rustling the leaves responded.

Sniffing the breeze, he tried to detect if the woman was still nearby. A delicious odor wafted toward him, masking all other scents and making his inner feline wriggle. *Catnip?* How strange.

Since the footprints ended here, he would have to investigate. He clambered down using his hands and feet. Descending as a mountain lion would've been easier, but approaching a frightened hiker as a predator was never a good idea, let alone one as rare as a mountain lion.

At the bottom, the strong essence of catnip made his feline instincts claw for attention. Reigning in his desire to shed his clothing and roll around on his back, he found the scuff marks of the woman's shoes and followed her trail.

Loose sand and random boulders made walking difficult, but the trail of catnip led him forward even when the footprints weren't clear. At a large tree, several limbs had been freshly broken, as if the woman had tried to climb up.

The scent of catnip was stronger here, as well as the delicious scent of female. Floral with a hint of sweet black tea, it reminded him of his early days with his mother, before his mountain lion had emerged, before the pack rejected him. A mountain lion didn't belong among wolves. He was what they called a "sport," an offspring with unexpected traits inherited from a long-ago ancestor.

The female scent in the area made his uniform trousers feel uncomfortably tight. *Mate*, his mountain lion purred. Adrian's balls agreed, but his head knew better. The catnip had to be messing with his senses. While he appreciated human females, he'd never met one who made him want to claim her. He was thinking about claiming this one sight-unseen.

And the heady scent was powerful, driving him forward even more than his duty to protect a hiker.

Ahead, another tree had four deep gouges staining the papery white trunk with lines of sap. *Claws.* This was a fresh bear marking. Adrian sniffed the air, senses muddied by warm female and dizzying catnip. The grizzly shifter had been here. Had made this mark. But something was off about the scent, a cloying, ashy odor that made bile rise in Adrian's throat. Randall's warning about an infection returned.

Running his tongue over his lengthening canines, Adrian unslung his rifle and unlocked the safety. The female ahead was in danger. *My female*, his cat rumbled. Adrian couldn't deny the instinct. He picked up his pace to a run...

Get UNTAMED INSTINCT now!

ABOUT THE AUTHOR

Once upon a time I thought I wanted to be a biomedical engineer, but experimenting on lab rats doesn't always lead to happy endings. Now I blend my nerdy infatuation of science with character-driven romance and guaranteed happily-ever-afters. My monsters always find their mates, with feisty heroines, tortured heroes, and all the steamy trouble they can handle. I promise my stories will never leave you hanging (although you may still crave more!)

When I'm not writing, I'll be in the garden or the kitchen, exploring Alaska with my husband, or preparing for the zombie apocalypse. I also enjoy crocheting while binge watching Netflix, playing video games, and enjoying family time during our weekly D&D session.

Interested in more about me? Join my VIP Club and get free books, notices, and other cool stuff!

www.tamsinley.com

bookbub.com/authors/tamsin-ley

goodreads.com/TamsinLey

facebook.com/TamsinLey

amazon.com/author/tamsin

www.ingramcontent.com/pod-product-compliance
Lightning Source LLC
Chambersburg PA
CBHW072134300726
48975CB00003B/1065